Berringden Br(

Life's Rich Tapestry

Jill Robinson

Berringden Books

Published 2012 by
Berringden Books

01422 883473

berringdenbrow@hotmail.co.uk

c Jill Robinson 2012

Cover design - Carly Surrall
carlysurrall@rocketmail.com
07533812474

For Ann Tillotson, Jane Springett and Suzanne Kendall

forty years on

Many thanks to Pat Neal and Tom Robinson for their editing skills and helpful suggestions

Chapter 1

Jess was not really enjoying the dinner party. The food was good; but the conversation, which had been dull and stilted throughout the evening, had now ground to a complete halt. Jess did not generally attend such events. It was one thing to have a few friends around for supper, in a relaxed atmosphere where everyone could be fairly sure of getting on with everyone else; however, this was a more formal occasion and Jess was a complete stranger amongst the guests, knowing no-one apart from her Canadian cousin, Jan. Hosts Dave and Barbara were Jan's best friends, and the dinner party was taking place in Regina. Jess liked Jan, she was a very kind woman, but they really had very little in common apart from the fact that they were step-cousins, sharing a formidable grandparent in Grandma Gladys. Jan had visited England several times over the years, but this was Jess's first visit to Canada, and she was feeling rather homesick.

A dog barked in a neighbouring yard, increasing Jess's feelings of nostalgia, since she was missing her own dog, Mash, at present being cared for by her friend Nick. The barking was the only noise in the dining room apart from the sounds associated with people eating and drinking. No-one, it seemed could come up with a suitable topic with which to restart the conversation. The lateness of the Spring that year had been thoroughly aired, and its implications and consequences for the wheat harvest had been discussed at length, throughout the starter and well into the main course. Now it was dessert and no-one could think of anything to say. However, the dog's barking now provided Jess with inspiration.

"I have a dog back home in Yorkshire."

Dave, the host, was sitting next to Jess. He smiled, and appeared glad of this new topic of conversation. "What sort of dog do you have?" he asked.

"She's a chocolate coloured Staffordshire Bull terrier. She's really sweet-natured. Her name's Mash - rather silly I know, but my son Alex chose it."

"And how old is she?"

"She's just seven. She's really gorgeous - she won the bonniest bitch competition at a local animal charity fun day last year."

There was an audible intake of breath and a resounding clatter of cutlery hitting fine china. Dave looked aghast, while the other guests stared silently at their plates - some crimson with embarrassment, others white with shock. Jess realised she had made a faux pass, but was not sure just how. Then it dawned on her that the cutlery dropping had occurred as she uttered the word 'bitch'.

"But that was actually the title my dog won. That's what we call female dogs in England. What do you call them here in Canada?"

"I suppose if you are using that word in that context." muttered Dave.

Meanwhile, Jan, her face pink with bemusement at her cousin's outrageous idea of what constituted suitable dinner party conversation, was looking around the room for a safer topic. Anything at all would be preferable to hearing another word about Jess's dog's beauty contest exploits. The setting sun shining through the conservatory window provided inspiration.

"Gee, Barb, how do you get your windows so sparkling clean?"

Everybody relaxed, and a thorough discussion of the opposing merits of commercial window-cleaning products versus home-produced remedies based on vinegar-soaked newspaper followed.

Of course, aside from this dreary dinner party, there had been aspects of the holiday which Jess had liked very much, for instance, the trip to the Rockies, the dip in the thermal springs at Banff, and afternoon tea at the hotel, overlooking the mountains. She had also enjoyed finding her way around her cousin's home city of Saskatoon by bus, when Jan had been at work. Jan had at first been horrified when Jess proposed taking the bus from the suburbs into the city centre.

"But my dear, I've never been on it, and I'm not exactly sure where it goes!" protested Jan, when Jess pointed out that there was a bus-stop right outside her cousin's apartment building. Jess had declared on the first morning that it was quite unnecessary for Jan to return home at lunchtime to fetch her, since she could easily make her own way to the hotel where Jan worked. Armed with Jan's mobile number in case of emergency, Jess caught the bus, finding that it crossed the South Saskatchewan River via the bridge right next to Jan's hotel. Jess spent some time at the nearby art gallery and the Ukrainian Museum, then walked round to the hotel and returned home with Jan, who was amazed at her independence.

The following day, Jess proposed a visit to the Museum of Western Life, again by bus, but Jan refused to allow this, insisting that she would drive Jess out to the other side of town. Jess spent the morning there, but afterwards, instead of ringing her cousin to be collected, as Jan had instructed, she had caught the bus back to the city centre. She knew Jan had an important meeting scheduled that for day, and could not understand her cousin's reluctance to let her explore alone. Jan had strictly forbidden her to go anywhere near the farmers' market, for reasons which remained unclear, but Jess found a small environmental centre near the river, which occupied her for an hour. Then she made her way back to the hotel, where she found that Jan had been telling everyone at the meeting how well her cousin from England was getting around the city, and maybe they should include something about the ease of bus travel in the hotel's publicity brochures?

Strangely enough, the highlight of this weekend in Regina had been a visit to the hairdresser who had always done her step-grandma Gladys' hair. Everyone joked that it was a "Long way to come for a hair-cut", which indeed it was, especially since Jess had not visited a hairdresser for five years, and generally cut her own hair, a fact which astonished Jan, who had her hair done every week. Jan had a rather annoying habit of making polite suggestions to Jess, such as "Did you want to brush your hair, dear?" before they went anywhere. Jess's hair was usually all over the place, because she did not use hairspray, or any other such preparation. As long as her hair was clean, that was all that really mattered to her. But now she was actually entering a hairdressing salon on the other side of the Atlantic Ocean... Anne's salon was located in the basement of her house, and Jess was intrigued by the procession of elderly neighbours who kept popping by to gossip, drink coffee and to meet their former neighbour's English grand-daughter. Each woman had a story to tell about the indomitable Gladys, and altogether the afternoon rather reminded Jess of the film 'Steel Magnolias'.

The following Monday saw Jess at the airport, on her way home. Her hand luggage contained a selection of bone china coffee cups and breakfast plates; the crockery had originally belonged to her natural grandmother, but had been purloined by Gladys. Jess's mother, Dotey, had long grieved over the stolen china, explaining that she had naturally expected to inherit her own mother's things; instead, her step-mother Gladys had taken everything with her to Canada, down to the last sugar-bowl. But now finally the chance had come for Jess to reclaim the family china, which fortunately, Jan and her daughters did not want. Sadly, Dotey had now been dead for more than thirty years, having predeceased Gladys. After Dotey's death, Gladys had had a fit of conscience and had confessed to Jess that she should not have taken the china, nor for that matter the family silver. Jess knew that her mother would have wanted her to bring everything back, and this was one of the reasons for her Canadian trip. She had been obliged to buy an additional bag to accommodate the extra hand luggage, and to obtain a large quantity of bubble-wrap. The silver cutlery had of course to be stowed in the hold - Jess wondered idly if anyone had ever actually attempted to hold up an aircraft with a set of Edwardian fish knives. The china arrived safely back in England, which was more than could be said for Jess, who had a hot cup of tea spilled in her lap over the mid-Atlantic.

"Oh dear, careless little me! I'm sorry, my love - this is only the second time this has happened in all my thirty years flying, "said the steward chattily, as Jess desperately tried to soak up the tea with an airline blanket.

"Well, it's the first time it's happened to me, and I hope it will be the last," said Jess, through gritted teeth, wishing that her spare jeans were not in her suitcase. She had not thought to include a change of clothes in her hand luggage. Her tummy and nether regions were now starting to sting. Calvin the steward thoughtfully provided some ointment for her to rub in, but there was nothing else she could do to make herself more comfortable apart from requesting another cup of tea to drink and waiting for the air-conditioning system to dry out her trousers. Meanwhile, she was obliged to sit in her knickers, hiding under the blanket. Luckily, the seat next to her was vacant, so she could move away from the wet patch. She wrote and complained to the airline afterwards, but never received any reply. Of course, Jess knew it had been an accident, but she thought that possibly she was entitled to some compensation - a few air miles perhaps. Her friend Nick met her at the airport and said she should report the matter to a "no win no fee" solicitor, but Jess was too tired to make a fuss. She soon forgot about the incident in her joy at being re-united with Mash, the bonniest bitch in Berringden Brow. sadly, the 'silver' fish-knives turned out to be merely EPNS.

Chapter 2

Jess was on her way to give a talk to a church social group in a village the other side of Leeds. Since she had written a book of short stories, she had been in demand as a speaker for local clubs and societies, and now her fame was spreading beyond the immediate environs of the Berringden valley, as her talks were amusing and everyone likes a good laugh. Jess had borrowed Nick's ancient Ford Mondeo, whose previous incarnation had been as a taxi and which still unaccountably smelled of old mops, since the village she was visiting was not on a train line. She had a pin-board with her press cuttings, together with a box of books, and she hoped to sell a few copies during the tea-break after the talk.

Just as she was driving into the car park of the church hall where the talk was to be given, Jess realised that there was something wrong with the Mondeo; the steering suddenly became very heavy and the ignition light came on. Jess pulled into a space and jumped out. There was water gushing from the engine, and Jess knew enough about cars to realise that the fan belt must have broken. She got out her mobile phone and called Nick. To Jess's dismay, he told her he was not in any breakdown scheme, but said that he would send his mate Mo who ran a recovery business to collect the car when he had time. Meanwhile Jess should return home by bus.

Jess relayed this information to the church club secretary, who said that she had better tell the vicar, since her car would be left in the church hall car park. The vicar appeared from his office, and seemed to be all right with the arrangement. Jess gave her talk, and a kind club member drove her into Leeds so she could catch the last train back home, the buses having finished at tea-time.

The following week, Jess received a call from the vicar, complaining that the Ford Mondeo was still in the church hall car park. Jess apologised, explaining that it actually belonged to her friend, who was arranging for it to be recovered. She had returned the car keys to Nick to pass on to Mo so that he could fetch the vehicle. Meanwhile, there was nothing further she could do. However, the vicar was not satisfied.
"You cannot duck your responsibility in this matter. You brought the car onto church property, and it is up to you to see that it is taken away," he barked, in a quite un-Christian way, Jess thought. After all, the car was

parked in a designated parking bay, it was not blocking the gate, and there were over forty spaces in the car park. She rang Nick again, and asked him when Mo was going to recover the Mondeo. "Um, when he gets around to it, said Nick, vaguely.

"But I've had the vicar on the phone, he's really cross. Can't Mo go today?" But Nick said Mo was too busy.

The next week, Jess had the police on the phone, acting on a complaint made by the vicar. She was surprised, and queried the necessity for police involvement, since this was clearly a civil matter. The car was not parked on the public highway and was not causing any obstruction. The police sergeant agreed. He was simply responding to the request by the vicar for help in getting her to move the car. On hearing that the Mondeo did not even belong to Jess, he rang off.

Another week went by, and the reverend gentleman's tone was turning decidedly unpleasant. He was threatening to scrap the car if it was not removed within seven days, and to send Jess the bill. Jess was by now becoming quite exasperated - with Nick for not being in a proper break-down scheme, with Mo for always being too busy, and especially with the vicar. It was only a Ford Mondeo, for heaven's sake, not a travellers' encampment. She felt like quoting the parable of the Good Samaritan, but in the end she merely remarked politely that she was glad that things were going so well in the village, as they clearly must be, if all that the vicar had to worry about was Nick's old car. Was he quite sure there were there no sick parishioners in need of a pastoral visit? The vicar rang off.

Nick eventually rang to say that Mo had promised to be available the next day. Nick had also had the police on the phone, they must have obtained his details from the DVLA computer, using the car's registration number. Nick said the police were very nice, pointing out that it was not a criminal matter, but it seemed they were becoming as fed up with the vicar's constant calls of complaint as was Jess. The Mondeo was finally recovered after its sojourn in the remote village, and the fan belt replaced. Jess decided to accept no more far-flung speaking engagements until she had her own reliable transport, and membership of a 24 hour recovery service.

The car had been returned to Berringden Brow just in time, it seemed, since on Sunday night, Jess received an urgent message from her younger son, Alex. "Mum, come to Hebden Co-op, asap, bring the car and lots of bin-liners. The freezers have failed and there's tons of food going to waste..."

Luckily, Jess had not had any wine with her evening meal, so she grabbed some bin-bags and drove the short distance to Hebden Bridge. The rainy streets were deserted except for a few shadowy figures with large rucksacks and laundry bags, hurrying towards the Co-op. In the unlit car-park Jess found a hive of activity, with people retrieving goods out of an enormous skip, and tossing them over the security fence, while others ripped off surplus packaging and sorted the food into different piles. The now defunct freezers had apparently contained mostly ice -cream and pizzas. Jess was just wondering how the food recyclers had managed to climb over the high spiky fence, when Alex appeared, walking along the low wall by the river. This evidently provided an easy route into the otherwise secure compound.

"Hi Mum, did you bring the bags? We've got to take some food parcels up to Bright Street, let's get going before the cops arrive..." Alex loaded several sacks of pizza into the car, and directed Jess towards the top of the town. Bright Street was a terrace of back-to-backs where people still hung washing across the road from house to house, and there were several sheets flapping dankly in the breeze. Jess was concerned that she would not be able to drive down the road without getting the laundry dirty, so she made Alex get out of the car and hold the sheets to one side while she drove cautiously towards the houses which were expecting the pizza deliveries. Despite her efforts to take care, Jess was startled by a stray pair of trousers, whipping against the windscreen, like a scene from "Get Carter." She had not noticed them in the dark.
All along the street went Alex, knocking on doors and handing in bin-bags of food to grateful recipients. Back home, Alex tucked into pepperoni pizza, while Jess quickly re-froze the ice cream, hoping that nobody would contract any strange diseases as a result of the night's endeavours.

"It's OK, skipping," said Alex. "My friends do it all the time; after all, Hebden's supposed to be a Transition town..."

"Remind me what that means," said Jess, emerging from the freezer.

11

"Um, one which lives in harmony with the environment, tries to live in a sustainable way, has a low impact, re-uses scarce resources, recycles...."

"Oh well, we've saved a lot of food from going to land-fill tonight, and those pals of yours seemed really glad of it, I guess it all helps eke out their unemployment benefit."

"Yeh, right; and thanks for helping with the deliveries. That's your contribution to the 'Big Society', Mum. Nice one!"

Jess was not sure that skip-diving was quite what the Prime Minister had in mind when he launched the Big Society campaign, but volunteering can take many forms, and she was glad to have done her bit. To her surprise, more free food arrived the following day in the shape of three-quarters of a large bag of strong plain brown flour, donated by Jess's neighbour Kate.

"It's kind of you, but I don't bake my own bread," said Jess.

"Don't you? Well, you really should start, it's much better for you than the shop-bought variety, and as for the taste, there's no comparison!" said Kate.

"Well, since you do bake your own, why are you giving me this flour?"

"Adrian's developed an allergy to gluten, so I have to use special gluten-free flour, but I already had this in and I really don't want it to go to waste."

"But I'm not sure I'll have time to bake, I'm just about to start a new job..."

"Well, it will simply be wasted if you don't use it and that would be a crime what with so many hungry people in the world, and I really don't know of anyone else I could give it to. You really should try to make time to use it."

Seeing that Kate was going to leave the flour with her anyway, Jess put the unwanted packet in the cupboard, next to the tin of Complan Kate had foisted on her when Adrian was ill and the doctor had prescribed it. Adrian had eventually tired of Complan, and declared he would take no more. Kate had insisted Jess and Alex use it, though neither required building up, quite the opposite in fact, and Jess was still on the lookout for a needy invalid who could make good use of it before its 'consume-by' date arrived.

Chapter 3

Jess had a new job. The neighbourhood advice centre, which she and Nick had managed for several years, had finally run out of funding and been obliged to close, and Jess had found work as a university researcher. Her task was to interview care home residents for a life history project.

It was of course necessary for Jess to have reliable transport to reach the care homes, which were located all over the county. Nick suggested a likely car that Mo was hoping to sell. Jess went to look at it, but it seemed too sporty for her. She contacted her insurance company, and asked how much it would cost to insure. The company rang back to say that they would actually decline to insure this particular model of car, since it was classed as a 'hot hatch'. Jess was not sure what this meant, so the adviser patiently explained that this type of car was judged to be amongst the most likely to be crashed or stolen, and was usually driven by a certain sort of young man.

Mo was scornful on hearing this news. "You need to change your insurance company, Jess. Is it one of those specially for old biddies? My cousin, he's in motor insurance, and he can get you fixed up, no problem!"

Jess explained that she wanted to stick with her present insurance company, which offered discounts for old biddies, so Mo took her round to his uncle's house, where there was a sedate-looking Nissan Micra for sale. The deal was done, and Jess drove happily home.

Jess was visiting Arnold, a family friend, who had Parkinson's Disease, and was now living in a care home. It was some months since his worsening condition had made it impossible for him to manage by himself at home. None of his children were able to care for him, so he had gone into a Nursing Home not far from where Jess lived. Mash was welcome to accompany Jess on her visits, since some of the residents missed the companionship of their pets, and the chance to stroke a friendly Staffy was considered to be beneficial. Arnold liked to reminisce about Sam, his family's dog; one of his favourite tales was about the time Sam had run away when the family had been on holiday in Shropshire. He had been found after an anxious twenty-four hours, at a remote farmhouse in the Longmynd, where the farmer's female collie was apparently in season.

Jess kept Mash on a lead and wearing her full harness when on these care home visits. Dogs were allowed to visit only in the conservatory, and residents had to go there to see them, so that other people who disliked dogs or who were allergic to pets could stay safely in the day room. As word went round that Mash was present, a procession of dog-loving residents and carers made its way to the conservatory, some in wheelchairs and others using walking frames. Mash enjoyed these audiences, always behaving beautifully. She was also a good topic of conversation, in an environment where the routine was such that nothing much out of the ordinary ever seemed to happen. Certainly, Arnold never had a great deal to say, but he enjoyed listening to the radio, especially the cricket, and particularly if Yorkshire were playing. Jess often found him alone in his room, but she was always perplexed by the strange noise coming from the room next door - almost like a duck quacking. When she asked what it could be, Arnold explained that the poor lady in the adjacent room was demented, and seemed to imagine she was a duck, so spent the day continually quacking.

Jess described her new job to Arnold, who agreed to act as the project's pilot study. The interview was conducted over two visits, because Arnold became tired, although he was determined to finish telling his life story.

"I was born in Loftus, in the North Riding of Yorkshire in 1928, and grew up during the Depression. I was the youngest of eleven children, and by the time I was born the two eldest had already emigrated to Australia, so I never met them until after the war. I left school at fourteen, and went into the office of a local mine, but times were hard, the iron ore mining was in decline, and I decided to try to train as a teacher. I went to night school to get the necessary qualifications, and eventually I was offered a place at Teacher Training College I was the first one in our family to go to college. However, I had to wait before I could take up the place until I had done my National Service. I was stationed at Pontefract Barracks. I met my wife June at a dance at Saltburn during one of the college vacations. She lived on a farm. She came from a large family, like me, and her parents had her marked down as the girl who was going to stay home and look after them, because she was the plain one of the family. It was quite a shock all round when we said we were getting married, but there was nothing anyone could do about it, as we were both over twenty-one. Parents often used to make you wait until you came of age in those days, unless there was a baby on

the way of course, when they would more or less have to agree. June wasn't expecting when we married, but she had a baby nine months later, a honeymoon baby. Unfortunately, it was stillborn, a little girl. The doctors said it was because of June's high blood pressure. I had qualified as a teacher by then, and I got a job in Leeds, so we moved to Cross Gates. June became pregnant again, and was closely monitored throughout the pregnancy. A little girl was born the following year, our Colleen. Everything seemed to be going well, so we decided to try again, to complete our family. We had a baby boy, but sadly, it was another stillbirth. We decided that we simply could not put June through all that again, and went for adoption. We got Neville through a church adoption agency. He had been born to a married woman who had had an affair, her husband said she could come back home if she put the baby up for adoption. She and her husband had other children, so that's what she decided to do, for their sake.

Then June accidentally became pregnant again. She was ill all through that dreadful winter of 1963, and our Andrew was born two months premature, he had to be induced because of June's high blood pressure. He was born with a degree of cerebral palsy and autism, but this was never properly diagnosed, not until we had him assessed privately years later, when we could afford it. At school, he was classed as ESN, 'educationally sub-normal', as they called it then. He was especially keen on history and for some reason, he had a great interest in despots and dictators, people like General Idi Amin, Emperor Bokasso and Napoleon. He knew all there was to know about them, yet he couldn't find his own way to the bus-stop; it's strange, isn't it? Some people affected by autism are very gifted, perhaps artistically or musically, and when June and I went to see the film 'Rain Man' with Dustin Hoffman, we came out and said to each other, 'That's exactly like our Andrew!' If you've seen the film, you'll remember that the Rain Man character was wonderful with numbers. Meanwhile, my elder brother and sister had visited us from Australia, where they were doing well, and they wanted us to visit them there. Of course, it was impossible while the children were young, we could never have afforded the fare on my teacher's salary. So we delayed the trip until I took early retirement; the children were grown up by then, although Andrew will never be able to function independently, he'll always need care. Colleen and Neville looked after him while we went on this holiday of a lifetime for two months. It was while we were away that our dog, Sam, died. Then, soon after we returned home, June was diagnosed with cancer. She lost an eye, but she was so *brave, as I'm sure you remember, Jess; she went back to work after a few months and carried on with one eye. Eventually, they said she could have a glass eye fitted, and it was such a good match, you'd never really notice if you didn't already know. But a few years later, the cancer came back, this time it was in her liver, and she died in 1991. It's hard to believe she's been gone so many years. I suppose you could say I never got over it. Colleen had moved away with her family, and Neville went to work abroad after he split up with his wife, so I don't see my grandchildren very often. Andrew visits every week, the carers bring him over from his home, it's for younger adults, and he likes it there, which is a great relief. We would never have got him a place without help, because he had to be receiving a certain benefit, and he was turned down at first. He was successful on appeal. Well, I'm sorry this has taken so long, I only talk slowly; it seems an ordinary story to me, but then most people would say that. No-one thinks of themselves as being special, do they, because it's just the life they've lived."*

Chapter 4

Jess was away for a few days visiting her elder son Tom in Bristol, Tom had planned a day out, "To see some people in Somerset," he explained.

"What people?" Jess wondered if Tom was taking her to a commune. You could never really be sure in Somerset. All that mystic Avalon stuff....As if reading his mother's mind, Tom told her to head for Glastonbury. They passed Worthy Farm, site of the annual rock festival, before arriving at the Tor. They climbed up and spent some time looking out over the magnificent view. Jess wondered if Tom had arranged to meet some friends here.

"Where exactly are these people we've come to see?"

"Oh, a bit further away, in that direction," said Tom, vaguely waving his arm in the direction of the Somerset levels.

"Well, what time are they expecting us?"

"Hmm, around dusk, I think...perhaps a little before. Not yet, anyway. We've got time to go and look at the Glastonbury Thorn, if you like."

"I first came here on a school field trip, about 1967," said Jess. "But that's more than forty years ago now! We went to Wells cathedral and Glastonbury Abbey. But just who are the people we're going to see ?"

"Um, Mr. and Mrs. Starling," replied Tom. "They live somewhere over there, in the Somerset levels. We should have brought binoculars."

By now, Jess had realised that they must be going to see the huge flocks of birds which congregate at dusk in the Somerset reed beds.

"I don't expect they'll be ready to receive us for an hour or so though."

"You're right, Mum; so let's have a cup of tea while we're waiting."
Tom consulted the map while Jess poured tea from a flask. Tom had looked at the internet where updates on the birds' roosting areas were published, so they headed for one of the villages named on the website.

"This must be it," said Tom, indicating where several cars were parked.

They left the car and followed the path through the reed beds, around a small lake, and eventually reached a wooden hide. There were a few people already inside, gazing intently over the lake, binoculars at the ready. After waiting for ten minutes in silence, a dark cloud could be seen approaching across the levels, continuously changing density and shape; the display – a mumuration – lasted several minutes before a loud swooshing was heard as thousands of starlings flew into the reeds.

"What a marvellous sight!" Jess exclaimed.

"Yea, great," Tom agreed. "I'm glad we saw them, Mum; you can never be sure from day to day exactly where they'll turn up."

"Not as many tonight as last night, though," said one man, dourly.

"And not nearly as good as it was at Burtle last week," said another. "Quite disappointing in fact. And you're all the way from Yorkshire? Hardly worth leaving home for. Well, I'm off to watch Corrie..."

Jess took no notice of the grumpy man, after all, it was not a competition to find out who had seen the most starlings

"How did he know you were from Yorkshire?" asked Tom.

"He didn't, he thought you were. You've still got your accent."

"Oh, yes, I suppose I have. And you've still got a bit of your West Country one. Funny how we've changed ends, so to speak..."

"Well, your feathered friends did not disappoint me, Tom; I've never seen anything quite like it. Thanks for a great day out!"

Chapter 5

The following day, Jess drove down to Devon to visit her old history teacher, Vera, in her retirement flat near the river. Vera had been in charge of Tiverton Grammar School library, where Jess had been a pupil librarian all those years ago. Now the Grammar School was a thing of the past, and most of Vera's colleagues had died, as, sadly, had several of her pupils, some much younger than Jess. Vera had never married, because professional women were required to give up their jobs upon marriage in those days, when a marriage bar had operated in many occupations including teaching and the civil service. Jess's mother, Dotey, had been obliged to give up her job as a telephonist upon her marriage in the 1930s.

Jess was bringing Vera a copy of her book of short stories and a potted plant, as it would soon be Vera's ninetieth birthday. The conversation proceeded over a cup of coffee, with Jess enquiring after various local residents whom Vera might have seen at church, and Vera telling her how many of them had passed away or were ill. Jess was shocked to learn that the young son of Gilbert, her first boyfriend, had died of a hidden heart condition, and that Miss Patrick, the seemingly indomitable maths teacher had also recently passed away, aged in her nineties. Jess prattled on about Alex's exploits, and also reminisced about the history trip to Glastonbury, which she had revisited the previous day with Tom. Vera shook her head.

"I couldn't even get to Exeter, these days. The journey would simply be too much for me," she sighed.

Jess did not stay too long, as Vera had a lunch club at the community centre to go to at noon. Jess was pleased to hear that there was something for the old folk to look forward to in the middle of the week. She was also very glad that the iniquitous marriage bar had been abolished by the time she herself had started teaching, so that she and other women of her generation had not been required to choose between a career and a family.

Jess left Vera's retirement complex and headed up to the car-park beside the canal, where she ate her packed lunch. Then she wandered up onto the tow-path, and soon found herself passing opposite the house where she had lived for fourteen years. This walk along the tow-path and around the lanes, past an ancient beech known as the Wishing Tree, had been a favourite Sunday afternoon stroll for Jess and her mother, after the ordeal of Sunday lunch was over. Jess's father, Jack, had been very particular about the way his food was cooked and served, he liked the beef to be rare, and would be severely critical if it was even slightly overdone. The trouble was that he liked to go to the pub before Sunday lunch and if he returned late, as he frequently did, Dotey would be struggling to keep the meat hot without overcooking it. It was the same with Jess's Yorkshire puddings, the bane of her teenage life; when Jack arrived late at the table the puddings would have sunk, or become burnt or soggy. It was not an easy meal to keep waiting. Jack always insisted on food being placed in serving dishes on the table, rather than dished up quickly in the kitchen, everyone had to hand the dishes around, making sure that Jack was served first. The meal was generally becoming cold and past its best by the time everyone was actually ready to eat. Jack would taste the first mouthful critically, and make a pronouncement. Jess always dreaded this moment, because her Yorkshire puddings were often unpalatable, and Jack would not spare his criticism. Once or twice Dotey tried to intervene, with a remark along the lines of Jack having come home rather late, although the puddings had looked wonderful at one thirty, his expected time of arrival. Jack would brook no answering back from any family member, especially the women, whom he regarded as little more than domestic servants, so Jess and Dotey learned that the only thing to do was to suffer in silence. Both would be longing for the meal to be over, and the dishes washed up and put away, so they could finally escape and snatch a couple of hours out of the house.

Jack was especially keen on Jess learning how to cook and serve food, explaining that the way to a man's heart was through his stomach, and that Jess would need to improve her domestic science skills considerably if she were ever to stand any chance of catching a husband. This would have been almost funny if he had not meant every word. To this end, Jess was also required to produce a sponge cake for Sunday tea, but that never seemed to turn out right either. Jack said that she could not have dried and sifted the flour properly, or whisked the eggs sufficiently, or beaten the fat and sugar mixture for long enough, and had she made certain that the oven was at the correct temperature? She really must try harder next time. Jack did not believe in praise, he was of the opinion that it induced a sense of complacency. It was his contention that criticism spurred the recipient on to do better. He could not accept that his continual carping was making Dotey and Jess increasingly more despondent.

Turning back down Canal Hill towards the town, Jess was by now walking right past her old home. She recalled how Dotey liked to gather Jess and her three bothers on the front steps to have their picture taken. Many years later, Jess had been visiting Tiverton with her two sons, and had sat them on the same steps for a photograph. She had knocked at the front door to ask permission from the current occupants of the house, but there was no reply, and it seemed that they were out. Just as Jess was taking the picture, the man of the house drove up. Jess had explained and apologised, but the man had been very good about it, and told her she could take as many photographs she needed. Meanwhile, eight year-old Tom had started to look rather uncomfortable, and toddler Alex was stoically sucking on his dummy, so Jess quickly ended the impromptu photo-shoot, and thanking the man again, had taken the boys off to the Wishing Tree, to run around and make their wishes. Jess had eventually written a short piece for the 'Guardian' newspaper, recounting the event. However, as Jess was now passing the house with its mixture of memories, a man dressed in overalls emerged from under the bonnet of a Land Rover parked outside the front door. Jess smiled, as she realised it was the same man who had allowed to her take her boys' picture on his steps. He peered at Jess, and recognition dawned.

"You're the woman who came here years ago with two little boys!"

"Oh, that was such a long time ago; the boys are quite grown up now."

"Well, I'll just get Joyce. Wouldn't you like to come in and look around your old home?"

"Oh, that's very kind, but I really don't want to inconvenience you ..."

But the man was now wiping his oily hands and calling down the hall.

"Joyce, that woman who used to live in this house is here again; she brought her boys to have their photo taken, about twenty years ago..."

A puzzled-looking lady appeared. Jess introduced herself and apologised for the intrusion, while the man quickly returned to mending his vehicle. The woman's face relaxed into a smile, as she ushered Jess into the house. "Yes, I remember Derek telling me at the time. Where are the boys?"

Jess explained about Tom being a surveyor, and Alex having the offer of a college place in Plymouth this autumn. Joyce was putting the kettle on, and insisting that Jess go through to see how the view over the valley had changed. Although, it was really remarkably similar, just several more houses, and the new road in the distance, but essentially the same outlook which had provided the background to Jess's formative years. The tulip tree which Jess and her brothers had climbed was still there at the bottom of the garden, although her father's kitchen garden was now herbaceous borders.

However, the interior of the house was completely different from the draughty barn-like place it had been in the 1950s and 60s. The new owners had installed central heating, new windows, parquet flooring, a fitted kitchen and a downstairs cloakroom. Jess mother had had to make do with a utility kitchen cabinet to store food, and she could only dream of possessing such items as a fridge or a washing machine. Jess's family had rented the house for fourteen years, during which it had been a real struggle to heat the place with coal fires and paraffin stoves, and there had been only an electric immersion heater to provide hot water. Jess remembered being limited to one bath per week. She was longing to ask if she could go upstairs and look at her old room, but felt that this would be too much of an imposition, so she drank her tea, thanked Joyce once more, and explained that she must return to the canal car-park before her parking ticket expired.

"Another time, you leave your car here" said Derek, emerging once more from beneath the Land Rover. "No need to pay to park."

The kindness of strangers, thought Jess, as she continued on her way. She had really enjoyed her trip down memory lane. Joyce had explained that she and Derek had come to the house as a young married couple, they had brought up their family there, and they had also converted the basement into a granny flat for their elderly parents. They were understandably loathe to leave the place after living there for so long, even though it was really too big for them now. Jess's own recollection of the house was of course clouded with many unhappy memories, centred on Jack's drunken rages, and his unremitting criticism of his family members, so it pleased her very much to think of the house as having provided a happy family home over the intervening years.

Chapter 6

Back home, Jess was pet-sitting for her friends up the road. Paul and Naomi were going away to their seaside cottage for a week and had left her in charge of their three cats and a pair of peacocks. The cats were generally no trouble, although one had a bad habit of catching baby rabbits, devouring most of the bodies and leaving only furry ears on the path. However, Jess was rather worried about the peacock, an arrogant creature, which liked to charge at dogs and people innocently walking along the adjacent footpath. The peahen was far more sensible, and tended to keep herself to herself; Jess often wondered how she put up with her ridiculous mate. Paul and Naomi's previous peacock had disappeared in mysterious circumstances one Christmas time, when it was feared that someone might have fancied a change from turkey, so Jess was anxious that this should not happen again. She hoped that she, the three cats and two birds would pass an uneventful week until Paul and Naomi returned.

On the second evening, Jess fed the cats and put some nuts and seeds down for the peacocks, of which there was ominously no sign. It was still light, and too early for them to have roosted. However, on returning home, Jess found a commotion in the adjacent street, where a group of neighbours was gathered round, gazing at two peacocks strutting along the roof ridge of the terrace. The male was giving his raucous call, and brazenly displaying to all and sundry. Altogether, it was quite a cabaret. Jess noticed that someone had left a skylight slightly open, and the peacock began rudely tapping on the glass and peering in; Jess hoped there was no-one dozing in the attic bedroom, since they might wake up thinking they were having a nightmare. Eventually, the exotic pair took off, and flew into a nearby tree to roost. There was nothing more to be seen that night, so the neighbours all went indoors. The following morning, after searching the immediate vicinity, Jess could see no sign of the birds. Just at that point, Alex clattered in.

"Hey, Mum, those peacocks are down the road at Sam's, in his hen-run; the male's displaying to the chickens, but they're not impressed. The peahen's just eating the chickenfeed. Sam and I did try to catch them, but they're crafty dodgers."

"This would happen the week I'm peacock sitting," sighed Jess. "But at least they're safe." She went to feed the cats, and trod in some rabbit entrails on the path. It seemed that one of the pets had been unable to wait for her arrival and had felt obliged to get its own breakfast. The next few days brought sightings of the peacocks from various locations in the neighbourhood. They were seen parading on the wall of the industrial estate; sitting in a tree in the woods by the railway; and perched on the chimney of the factory at the bottom of the road, looking for all the world like a pair of weathercocks. It had become known that Jess was nominally in charge of them, and people kept stopping her on her way to the shop, with the latest news of the errant pair. However, they always returned to Sam's garden whenever it was feeding time.

The birds were still evading capture when Paul and Naomi returned. Jess went to explain the absence of the peacocks, and Paul said he would go straight down to apologise to Sam, taking some bird food, since the peacocks were eating the chickens out of coop and run. All of a sudden, there was a strange rumbling noise, which turned out to be Alex, propelling a large black wheelie-bin across the yard.

"I've got the peacock! We threw a sheet over him in the hen-pen."

Alex opened the wheelie-bin and released the indignant captive bird. "Now I'd better go back for his missus."

However, this proved to be unnecessary, since at that moment a terrific honking noise was heard, and the pen-hen flew into the yard. The reunited pair flounced off into the shrubbery, while Paul went to fetch some of their favourite nuts and seeds, to welcome them home. Jess sighed with relief. Naomi went to put the kettle on, and Alex trundled the wheelie-bin back down the road. The peacock quickly resumed his duties attacking passers-by, while the peahen began to think about nesting, rather reluctantly, Jess noted; and with such an unreliable mate, liable to go fly-about at any time, she could quite understand why.

Chapter 7

Nick's mother, Eunice, had recently been admitted to a nursing home. She had been diagnosed with a recurrence of the cancer she had suffered from some years previously, and had for many months been struggling to keep Social Services at bay. She was afraid that if they became aware of the seriousness of her illness they would start sending carers into the house, and she did not want strangers telling her what to do. Nick, who still lived at home despite being in his late fifties, was out all day and most of the evening, on home visits to former clients of the advice centre, helping them to fill in forms for benefit claims, immigration sponsorship, tax rebates or anything else they wanted. Jess did suggest that he should spend more time at home with his mother, but Nick was not as good at taking advice as he was at giving it. He was very little help with household tasks, so Eunice's sister, Marigold, had been trying to do as much as possible, despite herself being in poor health. Eventually, there had been a crisis; Eunice had collapsed on the landing one night, and Nick had been unable to move her without causing great pain. Instead of calling an ambulance, Nick had left her lying on the landing, covered with a quilt, until the doctor's surgery opened at eight o'clock. The doctor immediately instructed Nick to find a place in a nursing home, where his mother could be properly cared for. A place was quickly found, and Eunice agreed to go in 'just for respite care.' Eunice, who did not realise just how seriously ill she was, frequently talked about what she would do when she 'got out of this place', which Jess found heart-rending when she visited with Mash. Eunice had left her house in a hurry, not realising that she could never return to live there. A social worker had informed her she could go home for 'afternoon tea' but just who would get the tea, wondered Jess; and would Eunice agree to return to the nursing home after the meal? Jess thought this would be very unlikely.

Nick suggested that Jess should get Eunice to relate her life story for the project, before she became any more ill; already her mind was clouded as a result of the drugs she had been prescribed, but she had expressed an interest in taking part. Nick phoned Jess one morning to say that his mother was having a better day, and wanted to talk.

My name is Eunice and I was born in 1921. When I left school, I went to work in the mill, like all the girls of our village. My father was the union representative for the local mill-workers. When I was seventeen, I began walking out with a neighbour, Raymond - he was a few years older than me. When war broke out, we decided to get married, because the future was so uncertain, he had been called up and was being posted overseas. I had to get consent from my parents, but they agreed, as they liked Ray.

Married women without children were also obliged to do some sort of war work, and I had a job as a post-woman, cycling all around the farms every day to deliver the mail. I have never been so fit, before or since! When he returned to this country, Ray was stationed at Hunstanton, so I went to stay with him there. It was lovely, by the sea, but a long way from home. After he was de-mobbed, he came back to Berringden and worked in a furniture factory. Then Nick was born, he had terrible eczema as a child and had to have coal tar treatments; he was in hospital a lot, and I wanted to be with him, so I never had another baby. I was so afraid that another child would suffer like Nick did. We got a dog, a black poodle called Sooty, and he became a playmate for Nick. Ray was a good craftsman, and also a good businessman, and he got promoted, so that he ended up as a company director for the factory. We had a beautiful house with a lovely large garden, we went on foreign holidays, to Austria and Switzerland; in those days you could actually take your car with you on the plane, so we flew over with the Jag and drove ourselves around.

We were able to send Nick to private school, but he did not like it, and once he ran away home. Ray took him back and insisted he stayed. We had high hopes for Nick, the teachers always said he was very bright; but in the end he did not pass his university exams and has not done as well as his cousin Roger who was at the same school at the same time. I put that down to the eczema, really; Nick never had much confidence because of it.

Ray became unwell, with diabetes and a heart condition, so he took early retirement. When Ray died, people said the house and garden would be too much, so we moved to a smaller house, but I've always regretted it. I think I had depression when I lost Ray, because normally I should not have let other people influence me like that. If only Nick had stood up for me! But he left all the decision-making to me, and of course, I was not used to it; Ray had always made the decisions in our family. I had to get rid of so much stuff, because we were moving from a large house to a much smaller one, and to tell the truth, there must still be boxes in the loft which have never been unpacked, even after twenty years. And there are things I've never been able to find, but must have been thrown out or given away.

I have two sisters, and they have several grandchildren - one has great-grandchildren now; they talk about them all the time, so I feel a bit left out because Nick has never had any children. He still lives with me -he's never wanted to leave. I would have loved a grandchild, but it was not to be. I'm a great-great-aunt, so I suppose I'll have to be content with that!

I began doing voluntary work at the Heart shop, you know, that charity shop opposite the library; I did that for years, right up to becoming ill. Even after I had to have a mastectomy six years ago, I still went back to the shop. I had not realised that the lump was cancer, because I'd had cysts in my breast before and they had been harmless, so it was such a shock when the doctors said I would have to have my breast off. I seemed to recover quite well, but now they say it is in my bones. I hope they can do something about it soon, as I'm sure Nick will not be looking after the house properly, and I really want to get back home and start some Spring cleaning....
Anyway, I hope this has been some help for your project. How's Mash, is she all right? I kept my mid-morning biscuit for her, in case you brought her with you. Perhaps she can come next time.

Shortly after Eunice had spoken to Jess Nick rang with the sad news that his mother had died. Her final words to Nick, who had been summoned to the nursing home by the night staff, were "have you called the police?" Quite what had been going through her mind, no-one knew.
Having always lived at home with his mother, Nick quite found it hard to come to terms with his loss. After the funeral, he and Jess began the daunting task of sorting out Eunice's possessions. Both she and Nick's

26

father had been terrible hoarders, and every room in the house was crammed with items of all descriptions, ranging from fur coats to used pan-scrubs. Nick's chief concern was to locate his mother's jewellery, which his aunt kept asking about. His mother had told Aunt Marigold that she was going to hide her rings somewhere an intruder would be unlikely to find them. "She mentioned putting them in a tin of talcum powder," said Nick's aunt, "or maybe Vim." Jess looked at the range of talc and scouring powders in despair, for Nick's mother had been in the habit of starting one and then opening another. Jess counted twenty-two tins of talcum powder and fourteen of scouring powders. She shook each one, in case the rings were hidden within. Nothing rattled, since the contents had set solid. Jess tossed the tins into the bin, whereupon Nick promptly retrieved them. "We can use it, don't throw stuff away!"

"No we can't! The damp has got in and it's all useless!" exclaimed Jess. "And I'm going to bin all these dishcloths, as well. Why on earth did she keep them, they're all in holes. And as for these worn pan-scrubs..."

"It's probably the war-time mentality, you know, 'make-do-and-mend'; she didn't like to throw anything out in case it ever came in useful." Jess was all for recycling and re-using wherever possible, but she could foresee no useful future for much of Nick's mum's stuff. Nick's father had left her comfortably provided for, so really there had been no need to hoard disintegrating dishcloths. But at least the Shelter shop was willing to take her collection of videos - the other charity shops seemed to have moved on to DVDs. Meanwhile, Nick was investigating the loft. He reappeared with an assortment of items including a macramé plant holder, a hostess trolley still in its box and a faded watercolour painting. "Guess what I've found up here?" smiled Nick.

"If you told me that you'd re-discovered the hanging gardens of Babylon I shouldn't be in the least surprised..."

"A bag of gold coins – Kruger-rands, I think. They were stuffed down beside the header tank. They were all the rage some years ago, my dad must have thought they were a safe investment."

However, Jess was more interested in the picture.

"This is nice. Look, it's signed 'R.G. Goodman. Wedding procession, Oudipur. 1903.' I wonder if it is an original? I've never heard of R.G. Goodman. But why didn't your parents have the painting on display?"

"Perhaps they didn't like it," said Nick. "Or maybe – I remember when the Chapel closed down, my dad was a trustee, they had to clear everything out before the building was sold for apartments. Lots of stuff was thrown into a skip; maybe he took a fancy to the picture and rescued it, but dared not have it on show in case a visitor recognised it."

Jess decided to take charge of the painting; she intended to do some internet research on the artist. She found that he had been born in England, but had worked mainly in South Africa. He was a prolific artist, and had exhibited at the Royal Academy. He had travelled to India twice, and painted many scenes of Indian life. Maybe the Oudipur wedding picture had formed part of this exhibition. Nick could keep his Kruger-rands, thought Jess; the painting was far more interesting.

Returning home, Jess discovered a large plastic bag in her shed. Kate had been clearing her wardrobe and decided that Jess was in need of her cast-offs. Jess was looking through the clothes when Kate appeared, telling her what good quality the skirts were, they were all lined and some were designer labels. Kate had recently put on a bit of weight, but this size should fit Jess.

"Thanks, but I don't really wear skirts, trousers, are warmer."

"Jess, we can't waste them! If you really can't use them, they can go to charity – you can take them to the Pop-In shop when you're next going. I simply don't have time, I have Adrian to see to, but you're a free agent. How nice that must be!

Chapter 8

I was christened Margaret, but I'm always called Madge, Margaret is my Sunday name. I was born in 1920 in a pit village in County Durham. I went into service when I left school, like all the girls did, the boys went down the pit but there was nothing in the village for the girls to do, so we had to look for work elsewhere. I was lucky, as my elder sister had already come to work in Leeds, and she heard of a place to suit me. I went as a servant to a Professor and his family, and they were very good to me. I was the maid of all work, well-to-do people still kept servants before the war. They lived up Roundhay, it was a lovely house. I was always a very good worker, there was never any dust to be seen, I kept things spick and span. Then on one of my half days -we had three half days every month you know, that was all the time off we had - that particular half day, I went to visit my sister, she had married a miner by this time, and was living at Micklefield. One of her husband's friends was there, he was helping Fred make a new pigeon loft. His name was Wally and we started walking out. We got married the next year, and naturally I left my place and moved to Micklefield. The war had broken out, and Wally was in a reserved occupation, being a miner. I went to work at the nearby camp when women without children were called up, but then I fell pregnant with my eldest. He was born in 1942. I was busy at home with him then, but it was hard managing, what with all the shortages. Wally kept an allotment and some hens, so we were better off than many others .We lived in an over-dwelling up sixteen stone steps, it was hard work getting the pram up and down, and carting the washing to and fro to the line. I used to donkey-stone those sixteen steps, people took a pride then in how their houses looked, not like nowadays when some people let their gardens go to wild. I had a tub and posser for the washing - do you know what that is? You'll likely have seen them in museums, but we had to use them every week! Wally had to have his bath in front of the fire, this was before they brought in pit-head baths and showers. Every drop of hot water had to be fetched up the steps and heated on the range. In those days, the miners received concessionary coals, they had them delivered every month, the coals were tipped out on the street outside the house and had to be shovelled round the back and into the coal-bunker. I always got mine done right away after they were delivered, rather than waiting for him to come home, as the coals were in everyone's way, stuck out in the road; but some people never bothered about inconveniencing folks, they just left their coals out, until it suited them to fetch them in. I always swilled away the soot so no-one would be treading muck into the house. I've always been very particular. We moved after the war, because our house was condemned and scheduled for demolition; we got a council house in the village, and we lived there fifty years. I suppose there were things I could have joined, WI and church groups, but I always kept myself to myself. I liked to stay quietly at home, and make sure my family was properly looked after. Very rarely, I might get the train into Leeds, but only if I wanted something you couldn't get in the village, such as a new corset. We did go on holiday once to a cottage at Filey, but I couldn't get on with the cooker, it was electric, and the one we had at home was gas, so I didn't enjoy the holiday. I cooked dinner every day; I don't hold with take-aways and suchlike. We never left the children when they were little, not once. I would not have wanted strangers looking after them. After Wally retired, we would go to the Miners' Welfare for the pensioners' treat, and sometimes we went on the outings, but I was always glad to get back home. They would stop at so many pubs on the way home, and I was always tired out and longing for my own fireside and bed. Wally developed emphysema, lots of the miners had it, and of course he smoked, they all did then. But it wasn't emphysema, as it turned out, it was lung cancer. I nursed him, you never allowed your family to be sent away you kept them at home. After he died, it was strange without him. then I started having my own health problems and had to come into here, but I don't really like it. There's nothing like your own front door is there... the carers are nice, but they don't keep the place as clean as I would like. I always ask them to Hoover underneath the bed when they do my room, but they just giggle as if they don't understand because they're foreign. I get out a yellow duster and go over things after they've gone, My sons come and visit, and the grandchildren, and now I've got a great grand-daughter - her mother and father aren't married, My granddaughter says that's how everyone is these days. 'Living over t' brush.' as we called it. In my day folk weren't so brazen about a child born out of wedlock but try telling that to my granddaughter! But the main thing is that the little girl is happy, that's what I hope for her.

Chapter 9

Jess was on a crowded train at Leeds Station one lunchtime, on her way home. She had been interviewed on local radio that morning about her book of short stories, but was a little disappointed to discover that the presenter of the Morning Show had not actually read it, having delegated this task to a researcher, who had suggested some questions for him to ask her. Jess had picked up a copy of the free 'Metro' newspaper and was looking at the puzzle page, when a loud voice boomed at her. It was Alex's friend, Will.

"Hi, Alex's Mum! Look, there's Alex's mum over there, how ya doing? I've just got out of Armley this morning! Me girlfriend's had a kid while

I've been inside, look, I've got his picture here, whad'ya think, Jess, isn't he a grand little chap? So I'm going to go straight now, for my kid's sake."

Will lurched across and thrust the photograph under Jess's nose just as the train suddenly set off, almost tipping him into Jess's lap.

"Oh Will; congratulations," murmured Jess, wishing that the other passengers were not staring so at her in such an odd way. Will was an alcoholic and petty criminal. He had lived around the corner from Jess's previous house, and had frequently landed on her doorstep late at night, when his mother had thrown him out. Alex had always insisted that Jess take him in, no matter the lateness of the hour, because he felt sorry for anyone with nowhere to lay his weary head. Will was usually in a terrible state, and Jess's sympathies were really with his mother, who had her own health problems. But she had always found Will a sleeping bag and pointed him towards the spare room, and reminded him where the bathroom was. Then there would be the problem of getting Will up and about before she could leave for work and safely lock up the house. Often he was in no fit state to stagger any further than Jess's garden shed, where there was an old settee, on which he could complete the sobering up process at his leisure. Will had disappeared from the scene some time ago, and from his comments Jess noted that Will had lately been a guest of Her Majesty at HMP Armley. So, she and the Queen apparently had one thing in common.

Tom rang from Bristol to congratulate her on her local radio broadcast, which he had listened to via the internet, telling her that her voice had sounded clear and friendly, still with a slight Devonshire burr, even after all those years of living in Yorkshire. Jess knew what he meant. Just before last Christmas she had had occasion to visit a village near Huddersfield, where there was a café barge on the canal. Jess decided to get a cup of tea before returning home, but as she boarded the barge, it seemed to her that everyone put down their knives and forks and was staring at her. Thinking that she might have intruded into a private party, perhaps an office lunch party, Jess enquired whether the café was presently open to the public.

"Well, tha's not from round 'ere, is tha'!"called out an elderly man. To which Jess replied, "Why, is this a local barge for local people?" She was disappointed that nobody appeared to recognise the allusion, even though they were actually not very far from the fictional town of Royston Vasey…

The waitress assured her that the café was indeed open, so Jess sat down at a spare table. She was keen to see whether any new arrivals would be greeted with same stares and suspicious glances as she had been - indeed, she was wondering if she would be expected to join in; but as luck would have it, no-one else arrived during the time it took Jess to drink her tea.

The phone went, and Jess hoped it was someone wanting to book her for a talk, but it was a bank she had never heard of, wanting to speak to Roger Smith. Jess explained that there was no-one of that name living there, but the caller repeated back the telephone number he had dialled, which was definitely Jess's number. The caller then became rather cross, insisting that Roger Smith had said that this was his number, and wasn't the address 19 Berringden View? Jess assured him that it was not. She reached for the phone book and looked up Roger Smith of 19 Berringden View. His phone number also began with 88, but otherwise was completely different to hers.

"I've found Mr. Smith's number here in the phone book," said Jess helpfully. However, the bank person said they had to go on information provided by their customers, not on what some random person who wasn't even one of their customers told them.

"But he's given you the wrong number."

Jess was becoming fed up with this conversation, so put the phone down. It immediately rang again. A different person from the bank, a woman this time, was asking to speak with Mr. Smith about his overdue credit card payment. Jess explained the entire rigmarole again, and again, the bank woman insisted that hers was the number Mr. Smith had given them.

Jess decided to ring Mr. Smith, but he was quite short with her, denying all knowledge of the bank and said he had no idea what she was talking about.

When the bank rang again, still chasing Mr. Smith's late payment, Jess was becoming understandably furious. She decided to contact the Financial Services Ombudsman, but although the lady she spoke to was sympathetic, she explained that there was nothing she could do, because Jess did not actually have an account with the bank about which she was complaining and the FSA could only consider complaints from bona fide customers.

Jess rang the Smith's number once more, and this time got Mrs. Smith, who apologised and said that her husband had indeed missed his credit card payment and had given a made-up telephone number to get the bank off his back. Of course, he had not known the number belonged to Jess, but he had been desperate for the bank to stop pestering him. They had been ringing up to twenty times day before he told them he had changed his number.

"Yes, and now they are ringing me, even though I keep telling them that the whole thing is nothing to do with me! They won't accept instructions from someone who isn't one of their customers."

"Well, they'll probably get fed up with it in the end..."

"But I'm fed up with it already!"

Jess had one more card up her sleeve, the telephone 'Choose to refuse' service. She rang BT and asked if she could join the call-barring scheme. She was able to sign up immediately, and received a pin number to enter after any nuisance calls. The scheme would be free for a month.

The bank rang again from its offices in London, Leeds, Manchester, Bury, Durham, Peterborough, Leicester and Derby, but as soon as she put the phone down, Jess entered the choose to refuse pin number, and finally the bank ran out of offices whose number she had not barred. Whether Mr. Smith ever paid his credit card instalment, Jess neither knew nor cared.

Chapter 10

I'm Patrick, and I was born in 1920. I suppose nowadays that you would say I had a privileged upbringing; I went to boarding school and we had lovely long summer holidays, of course, this was before the war. An idyllic childhood is how you might describe it. I was called up when war broke out, but I refused to serve, I became a conscientious objector. You see, I had visited the battlefields in France, and believed war was such a tragic waste of young lives - and all for nothing. The Great War was fought for no good reason. Of course, the second war, against Hitler, had justification, but I stuck to my beliefs and became a 'conchie'. I was sent to Wormwood Scrubs in London. Terrible place. I still find it difficult to talk about it, and

I don't really want to say too much now. The shame my family must have felt, with me inside. I asked them not to visit or write. The authorities let me out later to do First Aid work in the Blitz, so I suppose I made my contribution in that way. But after the war ended I found that some people were very strange with me, when they discovered I had been a 'conchie'; luckily there were others, mainly Quakers, who understood and sympathised with my views.

In 1948 I went down to Cornwall on my bike, staying in youth hostels. There was a wonderful young woman running one of the hostels, her name was Elizabeth. I fell for her, and asked if I could write to her. She agreed, and that is how our courtship proceeded. Nowadays, we would simply have jumped straight into bed I suppose. So we wrote for two years, then we got married. I had in the meantime trained as an accountant, so was in a position to support a wife. We had three children, and travelled all over Europe, because we thought it was important for everyone to experience different cultures and societies, and hoped that through a degree of greater understanding, further wars might be prevented. Elizabeth and I had a wonderful life together for more than fifty years, but last year she died, and the children said I really must not stay on my own, so they found me this place. What can I say? It's not really 'home' is it? But the carers are nice enough, although the food's not very good. I simply accept my lot. What else I can do?

Chapter 11

"The Antiques Roadshow" was coming to Manchester Town Hall. Jess and Nick set off on an early train, with the watercolour painting by Robert Gwelo Goodman in a large plastic carrier bag. It was an overcast day, and Jess was glad that it was not an outdoor venue. As they approached the Town Hall, they saw a large queue snaking around the square outside. The stewards directed them towards the end of it, just as a few drops of rain began to fall. Luckily, Jess had brought her umbrella. The queue was moving at a reasonable pace, and they soon found themselves inside the lobby. Then there was a another queue to get up the stairs, where the recording was taking place, and once upstairs, there was queue to get into the right queue, which in Jess and Nick's case, was the one waiting to see a fine art expert. The BBC had assured everyone that, so long as they were in the queue before 4.30pm, they would be seen. Of course, the experts all had to have a lunch break, which they took in shifts, thus keeping delays to a minimum. The Town Hall staff had provided trolleys with reasonably priced snacks and drinks, but Jess had brought a flask and sandwiches. She and Nick ate their picnic on the grand staircase. There were lots of people like themselves, with works of art in carrier bags. Jess wondered if there were any Lowrys amongst them. A Mancunian friend had once told her that he had unwittingly knocked at someone's door, to enquire about the adjoining house, which was for sale. His knock had been answered by L.S. Lowry, and they had chatted for a few minutes, although the artist had been unable to provide information about the house for sale.

The time passed surprisingly quickly, what with the picnic lunch, then patrolling the endless corridors in search of the loo, and chatting to the woman next to them in the queue. Jess had been to the Town Hall before, long ago, to attend a conference on changes to the welfare benefits system; but Nick had not previously been inside the splendid edifice, and was impressed with the huge paintings, statues and wall hangings. Then there was the filming to watch. One jolly-looking man in the queue next to them was being recorded talking at length about his art deco ceramics, which the expert, (whom Jess thought looked like something out of a period drama, with flamboyant whiskers and an exuberantly checked suit) was enthusing about. Jess wondered if he had ever accidentally dropped a valuable piece, while turning it over to show the camera the marks on the back.

Finally, it was their turn to see an expert. He asked what they knew of the artist. Jess explained that it was only what they had been able to glean from the internet. It seemed that Robert Gwelo Goodman's South African work sometimes fetched considerable sums, but his Indian work was far less popular; however, with the boom in the Indian economy, the expert said it was likely that this area of his work would become more sought after. Then he asked how Nick had come by the painting. Nick explained about the loft.

"Found languishing in the loft - possibly from an old chapel clearance?" exclaimed the expert. "I like it! It's definitely an original. Of course, it has faded a bit over the hundred years since it was painted, and it needs a new frame. You say the old one was damaged? In the present market, it should fetch between £300 and £500; but you say you don't want to sell. In any case, I would advise hanging on to it, since the value is likely increase."

The expert did not ask to have the painting filmed, but Jess and Nick did not mind, they were pleased to have had an informed opinion of the picture. It had been a long day, and Jess was anxious to get home to Mash, so they made their way to the station. Once back home and with supper out of the way, Jess had hoped to get an early night, but just as she was settling into bed, she heard the back door opening and two people come in. Alex must have brought a friend. To her horror, Jess recognised the louder of the voices, even through slurred speech, as belonging to Will. Alex was trying to get him to keep quiet, but to no avail. Will came clomping up the stairs.

"Where's Alex's mum? I love, ya, Alex's mum. I've always loved ya!"

Will fell through Jess's bedroom door, and gave her a clumsy hug. Jess had leapt out of bed and was struggling to put on her dressing-gown. Mash, meanwhile, was barking and going crazy with delight at this unexpected late-night visit.

"Hey Will, come down here!" cried Alex. "I thought you said you were hungry? We'll cook those fish pies. Mum, would you like some fish pie? There's a load going spare in the supermarket skip, they'll only take a few minutes to heat up in the microwave."

Jess declined the offer of a midnight feast, but Mash was licking her lips joyously as the smell of cooking pervaded the house. Will lurched off to the bathroom, and Jess hurried downstairs to have an urgent word with Alex.

"Why bring him here, at this time? Don't say he's got nowhere else to go!"

"That's right, Mum, his girlfriend's thrown him out. I knew you wouldn't be very pleased to see him in that state, but he followed me here…"

"Well, you'll have to get rid of him! I know, you've got the key for Scott's house while he's working abroad, haven't you?" Alex nodded.

"Well, take him there. The last train goes just after midnight. Be on it!"

"But the fish pies are almost ready, I promised Will some supper, the poor lad hasn't had anything all day, well, nothing solid…"

"You've got twenty minutes before the train goes, take the food with you if necessary," whispered Jess grimly, as Will was heard descending the stairs. There was a commotion, as he tripped over Mash. Mash squealed, Will swore, Alex shouted, and Jess began praying that the neighbours would not start rapping on the wall. Meanwhile, Nick, who was staying in the attic bedroom, had unbelievably slept through the entire episode, which just goes to show how tiring a day out at the Antiques Roadshow can be...

Alex knew from past experience gained over many years that he could push his mother so far but no further, because at a certain point she would snap. Evidently, this point was about to be reached, "Eat up, Will, we gotta go!"

"Wha? Whassat? You mean we're not staying here?"

"Change of plan, mate, got to get to the station. Going to Sowerby Bridge."

Alex and Will quickly ate their fish pies and dashed to the station. Jess heard the midnight train arrive, and phoned Alex. "Did you catch it?"

"Yea, no worries, Mum; we're on the train now!" Jess sighed with relief.

Chapter 12

Shall I start speaking now, Jess? The tape-recorder is working is it? Well, here goes! I was born in Southampton, in 1925. My name's John. I'm a long way from home, and you couldn't get much further away from the sea than Berringden, could you – it must be about two hours in either direction. I miss it a lot, I really do, but my son insisted I must be near him. And now he's just died, he had cancer, it's not right to have your children go before you, you never expect it...and I'm stuck here, with no family. My granddaughter lives in Essex, and she's trying to get me moved nearer to her. She's in Clacton, that would be wonderful, to be by the sea again. I was in the merchant navy, it's true what they say, you know, about sailors having a girl in every port! I sailed all over the world, Singapore, Aden, Cape Town, Buenos Aires, San Francisco - you name it, I've been there. And enjoyed every minute of it. We mariners are very resourceful, you know, we can do for ourselves - sewing and that; and we keep things tidy - ship-shape, you'll have heard the expression. My wife always said I got under her feet when I was home on shore leave, and she was always glad when I was away sailing again. I was quite relieved as well...Now I have trouble with my waterworks and have to use catheters and they have to measure and analyse my water every day -there's no dignity to growing old, not if you're like I am now. When I think of how I used to be – handsome - yes, that's my picture, quite a sight for sore eyes, wasn't I? I don't have very much to tell you really, and it makes me sad thinking about it, so I'll finish now, if you don't mind. Just time for a nap, before those care girls come round with their blooming beaker for measuring my water. I hope not to be here next time you come - I mean I hope to be in Essex, not dead!

Chapter 13

Jess had received an invitation to attend a drama production from some old friends, a couple who had lived in Berringden Brow when their children and Jess's boys were small, and they had all belonged to the same babysitting circle. Michael and Clara's now grown-up son, Evan (one of the babies for whom Jess used to sit all those years ago) had actually written two one-act plays, which were to be performed in a pub in Salford.

Jess was not used to such an intimate venue, with the audience seated so close to the performers; she felt that they were almost part of the set. She hoped that the performances would be good, and that she would enjoy the evening, since she found herself sitting in between Evan the playwright and his mother Clara, who would be able to gauge her reaction.

Jess actually enjoyed the first play, which featured a woman trying to help people at a suicide black-spot. However, she had reservations when she returned after the interval and saw the set for the second piece, where two people, a man and a woman, were lying bound and gagged on metal beds. The play opened with the female character screaming in a piecing manner through her taped mouth, for what seemed an eternity; it was so harrowing that Jess wanted to rush up on stage and liberate her. Things got rapidly worse when the jailer appeared, a sinister creature, who kept up a black-humoured commentary. He was continually popping in and out, with cups of tea and a vacuum cleaner. There was only the one door, which was used to gain access to the auditorium, as well as the performance area. Finally, Jess could take no more of the woman's screams; she knew she must leave, despite being seated next to the playwright. She got up and crept out onto the landing, where she encountered the stage manager. He looked at her troubled expression and nodded.

"You're quite right to come out at this point; it only gets worse."

"You mean that screaming continues throughout the entire play? The poor actress must have a sore throat."

"No, actually, the screaming stops quite soon, but some even more distressing things happen…"

At this point, the jailer character appeared on the landing and dived into a store cupboard, from which he produced an enormous machete. He grinned at Jess as he stuck the machete down his tracksuit trousers and returned to the stage. Jess heard shouts and screams from the stage, followed by gasps and groans from the audience. Two other people rushed through the door and ran down the stairs in the direction of the toilets with their hands over their mouths. The stage manager again nodded at her.

"You see? It's getting very nasty in there! This play is really not for the faint-hearted.

"But Evan's mother told me that it's had really good revues and that he's planning to take it up to Edinburgh…"

"Yes; those member of the audiences who've managed to stick it out to the end have been most appreciative. The local reviewer gave it four stars!" Jess accepted that the best course was to remain quietly on the landing until the play ended. If she tried to return, she would probably faint or be sick; and anyway, if she went back through the only door, people might think she was part of the performance. Finally, she heard polite applause, and the audience made their way down the stairs. Many were looking rather pale and fraught and definitely in need of a restorative drink. At last, Evan and his parents appeared. Jess moved forward to apologise for having walked out, but Evan seemed quite relaxed about it.

"Don't worry Jess, we had three walk-outs last night as well. It is rather a challenging piece…"

"The performers were wonderful," murmured Jess, "from what I saw – and heard. In fact, I had rather an interesting perspective from out here, with the psychotic character coming in and out all the time. And of course, the first play was really thought-provoking, and the actress was excellent."

"It's OK, Jess, you don't have to keep trying to salvage something good out of a rotten evening…"

Evan was laughing good-naturedly at her, and she was relieved that he had not taken offence.
"Perhaps I should have warned you in advance that it was rather harrowing," said Clara.

"Jess didn't really stay long enough to see much," said Evan. "Just the screaming was too much for her."

At this point, Evan's father Michael suggested they all repair to the bar. Evan began talking about his next play, which he was still writing, featuring a hapless married schoolteacher's visit to a prostitute and the ensuing complications; the rating was likely to be 15, since the piece was set to contain sexual themes and some strong language, and Clara joked that they had better nail Jess's feet to the floor for that production.

Chapter 14

Hello, I've glad you've come to see me, I don't get many visitors. My sons live away, one is in Wales and the other is down South. My name is May, and I am 86 years old. I am not from round here, I've lived most of my life in the Cheshire area. I came to Yorkshire quite recently, and I'll tell you how it happened. A very nice young man came round to the retirement flats where I was living, he was selling these care alarms - you know, you press a button if you are in trouble, and someone comes to help you. I thought it was a good idea, with me being on my own and no family nearby, so I signed up for one. Anyway, the young man and I got talking, he really was very charming, and when he found out I did not have many friends he said he would he call back later that week. You see, the other people in the flats all liked playing bingo and doing the lottery and suchlike, and I had been brought up very strictly, our Chapel disapproved of gambling of any kind. So I could never really socialise with the other residents. John – that was this young man's name – said it was a pity I was lonely, and he suggested I should sell my flat and move to Berringden Brow to live with him. So that's what I did. There's always a demand for ground floor flats, so it went very quickly. We sold the furniture as well, because John said that there would not be room for it in his cottage. John said he would invest the money for me, and I moved into the back bedroom of the cottage, it was high up on the moors overlooking the valley, the views were wonderful. Of course, it was rather remote, and there was no bus route nearly, so I could not get out very much, but I occupied myself keeping house for John, I did all the cooking, cleaning and washing –by hand, as his machine had broken down.

John had told me that he was going to build an extension to the cottage with the money from the sale of my flat, so that I would have my own space, but one day when I was hanging out the washing I got chatting with the farmer up the lane, and he said that this would not be allowed because there was a public footpath at the back of the cottage, and John would not get planning permission to build over it, so I did not know what to think...I asked John about it and he said not to worry, it could all be sorted out.

Meanwhile, John had bought a Range Rover, and a pony for his children – oh yes, he has two children from his marriage, but his wife left him. John told me he had two other children, with a woman in Berringden, but I did not believe that he could possibly do anything as immoral as have children out of wedlock. That is why I fell out with my elder son –he and his wife adopted a baby girl, but I said to them, why ever do you want to do that, you've no idea what her background is, she might be the product of immorality !They did not take my advice and we've scarcely spoken since.

John's such a fine good-looking man! That's his picture, don't you agree, he's very handsome? That's his Scottish Country Dancing outfit, doesn't it suit him? He's away in Australia at the moment – but he'll be back soon.

You're interested to know what brought me in here? Oh well, I was feeling ill, and of course, I was not registered with a Berringden GP, so John took me to see his doctor. I told him the story of how I came to be in the area, and I happened to mention that I might be a little worried because John might not be able to build the extension he had promised for me, and the silly doctor got it into his head that I was depressed, and advised me to leave the cottage. All I needed were some antibiotics, but things got

41

completely out of hand, the doctor made an appointment for me to see a solicitor, and then the solicitor called the police, and they told me I had been the victim of a conman! Can you believe that, John- a conman? They made me give them a statement and then they went to arrest John and find out where my money was. He tried to run away over the moors, but they sent a helicopter to track him down. They actually handcuffed him, and he led them to a place among the rocks, and do you know, my money was all there, hidden away in plastic carrier bags! John said he doesn't believe in banks, and you can't really blame him after the Northern Rock and RBS scandals. The police made me go into a hotel, while they prepared their case against John; he was forbidden to communicate with me, but he sent his parents to see me, and they asked me to drop all the charges, so of course I did. I never wanted to bring them in the first place! The police were very cross with me and said I could be fined for wasting their time, they had to let John go, but I had never wanted them to prosecute him.

Anyway, they sent a lady called Anna, to see me, she was from some local befriending scheme, and she told me that she actually knew Imogen, the woman in Berringden who had two children to John, she said they were twin boys, but I still think she was making it up. She's been coming every week since John left for Australia after the police let him go, but I shall tell her not to come any more, because John will be back soon. He left quite suddenly, saying that he had business in Melbourne, and of course, I was homeless, so the social workers put me in here, they wouldn't let me go back to the cottage to be on my own because it was so far away from the village and I would have been stranded up there all winter with no-one to take me out shopping or anything.

Anyway, a busybody woman who runs the Friday lunch-club at the village hall told me that John had gone to Australia with a woman called Marnie, she is Australian but she had been living here for a year or so, and she did Scottish Country Dancing with John. Of course , I did not believe her, but then I actually got a postcard from Marnie– this is it, as you can see, it show two tree-frogs mating, imagine what the postman must have thought when he delivered it! She says that John is her husband now and I must forget him. But she is lying - see, this came in the next post, a letter from John himself! He says he will be home very soon now his business is completed. He's been away six months over the winter – their summer of course. He tells me to ignore anything I hear from Marnie, because she's *very prone to imagining things, of course I'd already guessed that; and he says that he and I will soon be together; I'll read you a bit, shall I?:*

"Darling May, not long to wait now, we will soon feel the warm Spring sunshine on our faces and hear the birds serenading us together in our little cottage in your own special month of May". Isn't that lovely? So I shall be getting out of here very soon!

Chapter 15

Paul and Naomi were away again for a few days, so Jess was cat and peacock sitting once again. Paul had also asked her to deal with any phone messages, since he had just sent out a consignment of magazines, which might possibly give rise to some queries. As Jess was switching on the answering machine, pen poised to deal with any enquiries, the phone rang. The loud voice of an irate magazine subscriber was complaining that he had had just received the latest copy, but that the envelope had a shit stain on it.

"I beg your pardon?" queried Jess in astonishment.

"You heard me right the first time! There's a very suspicious-looking brown stain right across the envelope. Now what have you to say about it?"

Jess knew that the magazines were packed in the kitchen, so went to look for clues. All became clear when she noticed a jar on the table.

"I think you'll find that it's Marmite," said Jess, as she put down the phone. She threw some grain down for the peacocks, who were strutting about in the yard, and fed the cats, who were all three dozing near the Aga – thankfully, the livestock was all present and correct.

Walking back home through the woods with Mash, Jess became aware of the smell of wood smoke and cooking meat. Mash licked her lips and scampered off in the direction of a leafy glade, where a group of men, two young and two middle-aged, were lolling around a camp-fire. They had rigged up a spit, upon which they were roasting a small deer. It was an almost medieval scene. The two younger men were wrapped in old woolly blankets, and one was idly strumming a guitar. By the time Jess arrived, she found that, Mash, ever the flirt, had made herself quite at home, lying beside a young man with dreadlocks, who was tickling her tummy.

"Hiya; grand little dog, ain't she? Me mate used to 'ave a Staffie, bit like her, not quite as dark a coat though," smiled the young man.

One of the older men looked at Jess rather doubtfully. "It's just road-kill, this, you know, love; found it lying by the side of Berringden Lane and decided not to waste it, like. It's me lad here's 18th birthday, so we're celebrating out here in the woods; me and him and his uncle and cousin – a proper men's day. Ray Mears and Hugh Fearnley-Whittingstall and all that stuff – much better than a pub crawl - brought some home-brew with us; what could be nicer? S'really quiet round here; we've hardly seen a soul."

"Well, you've got a lovely day for it," said Jess. "Congratulations, I hope you have a very happy birthday. Now, I'd better rescue my dog…"

She put Mash back on her lead, and made to leave, but the man seemed keen to continue explaining exactly what they were all doing.

"We've come down from Upper Berringden; nay, we're not all thieves and druggies and alkies and skivvers and scroungers up there, despite what folks might think. I used to roam the woods when I were a youngster, and I wanted the same for my lad. People were proud to work then, to support their families; now they seem to think working's a sign of weakness when you can sign on and deal drugs on the side or go on the sick. Not that there is much work to be had around here at the moment, what with all the factories shutting up shop and the brewery closing down…"

At that moment the peacock's distinctive call carried on the evening air, sounding so clear that no-one could fail to notice it. Jess was glad the men already seemed to have sufficient meat. The uncle, who had been slumped beside the fire, suddenly woke up, seemingly unaware of Jess's presence.

"A peacock sitthee! Well now, this must be the place where our Alf caught his Christmas dinner." The others were giving him warning looks and glancing meaningfully in Jess's direction, but the uncle went on, oblivious.

"T' were right tasty, that bird. He wa' very secretive about where he got it. And Mary did a right nice arrangement of the feathers in their front porch."

Jess hauled her reluctant little dog away from the convivial scene. The venison smelled like it was done to a turn, and all Jess had planned for supper was a mushroom omelette, and a tin of tripe dog food for Mash.

The following week, Jess had been asked to do a book signing in a chip shop, as a fund-raising event for AIDS charities. The shop was owned by her old friends Vic and Carmel, who had generously agreed to give a free fish supper to anyone who bought the book that night, and the event had been advertised all day on local radio. People came trooping in from miles around, and the evening was a great success. Jess reflected that it was possible to sell books in quite unexpected places; maybe the strangest had been the queue for the ladies' loo at the cinema where a neighbour's friend wanted something to read to while away the tedious minutes before a cubicle became free. By the time one was available, the woman was several pages into the book bought it. The trick, Jess had discovered, was always to have a copy to hand. Once at the launderette a man had too arrived to collect his wife's dry cleaning, he was sitting glumly twiddling his thumbs, and asked the assistant if there was anything to read. She shook her head but Jess seized the opportunity and produced her book from the depths of her laundry bag. The man immediately became engrossed in reading it, so that by the time the dry cleaning was available for collection, he was already on chapter three, and asked to buy it as a present for his wife.

Chapter 16

Hello, I'm Mildred, Milly they call me. I'm – oh, now you're asking – I was born in the General Strike, so 1926. It's been quite an ordinary life, nothing much to write home about. Although, we did go to Australia on those £10 tickets you could get. We thought it was going to be a better life, a fresh start in a new country. Well, it took weeks to get there by boat and it was such a relief when we finally arrived, but it didn't really work out. I loved it, but my husband found it hard to get work at first, and we had to live in these not very nice huts in a camp until he found a job. It was a bit primitive, but the fine weather made up for it after rainy Yorkshire. I had worked in the blanket factory and my husband had been in the chicken hatchery, they sent day-old chicks all over the country from Mytholmroyd station at that time. Why did we come back? Well, our families kept sending these really heart-rending letters, saying how much they missed us, and how hard it was with us on the other side of the world. And my husband never settled, he was more homesick that I was! To top it all, I fell pregnant, and my husband was fretting that unless we went home the child would not be allowed to play cricket for Yorkshire as players had to be born here. They've abolished that rule now, anyone can play; and as it turned out, that first baby was a girl. So we came back after two years, and we never went abroad again. My husband refused to set foot outside the country, in fact, it was a job to get him to leave Yorkshire. We went to Scarborough for our holidays -we did go to Blackpool one year, but he didn't care for it. I wanted to try Cornwall, but he said it would be too far to go. After we came back from Australia, we took a corner shop in Bradford, it was hard work, the newspapers came at crack of dawn, but after the failure down under we were determined to make a go of it. We had this particular customer, came in every morning, a nice-looking man, they called him Peter. I never knew his surname, but one day he didn't call in, the neighbours said the police had arrested him; it turned out he was Peter Sutcliffe, the Yorkshire Ripper, he murdered all those women! Thirteen in the end, some were prostitutes but some weren't, and anyway, what does it matter, a life's a life, however a woman earns her living. The last one was just a young student, with all her life ahead of her. None of us in the area ever suspected. Why should we? He seemed quite ordinary,

I started out by telling you that mine had been an ordinary life, and now I realise that not many people will have lived in Australia, or sold the Yorkshire Ripper his daily paper. All that small-talk, about the weather, or if they'd got the road dug up again... and of course, I would have made some comments about the headlines in the paper, something like "Oh dear, I see he's got another one". You always had to be pleasant with the customers if you were a shopkeeper. However, that Ripper business did it for my husband, he said he didn't want me on my own in the shop serving customers when you never know who's coming in. He was often in the stockroom or at the Cash and Carry, so we sold the shop and retired. I missed the customers, though, and it was a bit too quiet for me. My husband took up gardening, he would do everyone's garden, because lots couldn't mange it, or didn't want to be bothered, so I used to go for long walks around the hills, with the dog. Then last year my husband died, and so did the dog. I lost heart somehow, all on my own. I like it here, there's

plenty of company, and I've taken up something new –you're never too old
to learn. I went on a computer course at the library, for silver surfers, they
call it, and now I edit the residents' newsletter! I'm so proud of myself! I'm
always on the lookout for news items, it can be rather slow sometimes, so if
you like, I can put in a bit about you and the life histories project. That will
make a very nice item, and give you some publicity as well. What else do
we find to put in it? Well, we have a 'Births, Marriages and Deaths'
column; of course, it's mainly deaths, but we do put something in if one of
the carers has a baby. One had twins last month, she's bringing them in to
see us tomorrow, I'll take a digital photo for the newsletter. And last year
we had a marriage, two of the residents got together, although
unfortunately the groom did not survive long after the wedding. His widow
Myrna is still here, though, she's on the lookout for a new man now. I think
she was after John, he's been a bit of a ladies' man in his time, but now
he's got this trouble with his waterworks, and anyway, he wants to move
away to Essex so she's lost interest in him, I might introduce a 'Lonely
Hearts' column in the next issue. What about Speed Dating? I hear that's
all the rage now – maybe it's the perfect solution - we don't have so much
time left once we're in here, do we?

Chapter 17

Jess's friend April sent an email from London to say that she had won a
raffle prize, which turned out to be a free weekend at a hostel in Whitby, so
would Jess like to meet up with her on the Sunday? Jess and Mash set off
for the coast and collected April from the place where she was staying.
They walked up to the Abbey and sat admiring the view while they had a
cup of tea. Mash caused a commotion by becoming much too interested in
the remains of someone's sandwich, carelessly discarded on the grass;
however, an enormous seagull flew down and claimed it just before Mash
got to it, squawking fiercely at her. Mash retaliated by barking loudly, so
Jess had to run over, shoo away the seagull and put Mash back on her lead
in order to calm the situation.

They walked down the steps and through the town to the harbour, where a
retired lifeboat skipper was drumming up custom for his next trip round the
bay, in a decommissioned lifeboat. Both April and Jess were keen to
support the lifeboats charity, so they asked if dogs could go as well; on
hearing that Mash would be welcome, they boarded the vessel, which was

quickly filling up with trippers. The boat sailed peacefully towards the harbour mouth, but once out in the open sea, it began to pitch and toss quite alarmingly. April was clutching Jess's arm, while Jess was clinging onto her seat, with Mash quietly cowering underneath. April became quite upset. "Make his turn round, Jess; make him go back!" However, Jess did not see what she could do about it, since everyone else appeared to be enjoying themselves; Jess supposed they might be used to the thrills and spills of modern fairground rides, so this boat trip would be a quite tame by comparison. The skipper heard April's cries of distress, and gave her a reassuring nod.

"Don't worry, love; this is nothing! We'll be turning back once we've reached the buoy over there, and it won't be nearly so bad going back."

April was still clinging on to Jess, who was scanning the sea for sight of the buoy. To her relief, it was not far away so she relaxed. After all, the skipper knew what he was doing. Even so, Jess was glad when they rounded the buoy and began the return journey, sailing smoothly over the tops of the waves. Once safely back on the quayside, Jess and April rushed into the lifeboat shop, anxious to support the charity. However, Jess was immediately asked to leave, because she had Mash with her and dogs were not permitted inside the shop. Jess was rather surprised at this, since there did not appear to be a notice on the door, and it was not a food shop. The shop manager suggested that she tie Mash up outside, but Jess replied that her dog had actually been stolen once when left tied up outside a building in Hebden Bridge, and had been recovered only when Jess had raised the alarm and brought the town to a standstill. It seemed that the only way Jess could support the lifeboats was for her to wait outside until April had finished shopping when April could to mind Mash. It seemed odd to be buying Christmas cards so early in the year, but Jess bought two packs. They then wandered down to the beach, but there was a sign indicating that dogs were banned. Jess was becoming rather exasperated. So it seemed were several other dog owners, since there were actually quite a few dogs chasing around on the beach, blithely ignoring the sign. Of course no-one wants to step in dog mess, but if it is cleaned up and the dogs are kept on leads, then there is no harm done. Mash was looking wistfully at the sand and the sea; she always enjoyed a paddle. Jess knew she had the solution and rummaged in her rucksack.

"Oh dear, we can't go on the beach," said April, reading the notice, Jess, meanwhile, had produced Mash's stout leather harness and some reflective tape from her rucksack, and was busily engaged in the process of disguising Mash as an assistance dog. On the occasions she had used this ruse, she had never been challenged. Mash had gained entry to all manner of interesting buildings and picturesque gardens; Jess's tactic was simply to stride boldly towards the gates, smile pleasantly at the doorkeeper, pay the fee, and she and Mash would be waved through without question...Jess and Mash paddled in the shallow waves, under a glorious sunset. Then it was time to return April to her hostel in time for the evening meal, before heading back home to Berringden Brow. Mash at once fell asleep on the back seat, worn out with the day's excitement, and possibly dreaming of choppy seas, an alarming encounter with a seagull, eviction from a charity shop and the adoption of a cunning disguise in order to get onto the beach. Staffies lead interesting lives.

Chapter 18

Hello Jess, it's my turn to talk to you today, isn't it? My name is Sally – actually, it is Stavrula, as I'm from Cyprus. When I came to Britain people here found it difficult to pronounce Stavrula so I started using Sally instead. I have been here forty years or so, but I am hoping to go back to Cyprus soon. I'm only in this place because I'm convalescing after an operation, and I'm expecting to get out in a week or so. I have had four husbands – people usually look at me in amazement when I tell them this - a bit like you're trying not to do now - and I always think they must be wondering what I put in the cooking; but I have just been very unfortunate. Then there are the jokes about the Cypriot, the Englishman, the Irishman and the man from Lebanon- believe me, I've heard them all in my time. My four husbands all had different nationalities.

I married my first husband very young – it was the custom in my country in those days. I was only fourteen and had not even started my periods. I did not know what was happening to me – I had been told nothing! There was no sex education in my day. So I fell pregnant straight away and gave birth to my first daughter, Andrula, when I was only fifteen. My second daughter, Aphrodite, was born the following year. My husband, Andreas was one of Archbishop Makarios's bodyguards- Makarios was the Cypriot leader for many years. This was before the Turkish invasion of 1974 and the illegal division of the island. There were tensions between the Greek and Turkish communities, so Makarios had to be constantly guarded. Andreas was killed by an assassin, but of course, the Archbishop was the intended target, so my husband died bravely, doing his duty. I was left as a teenage widow with two tiny children, and of course I wondered how we would manage. My family helped, and then I met my second husband Geoff, at a dance at Akrotiri. The British forces maintained a number of military bases on Cyprus and Geoff was a serving British soldier. After his tour of duty finished we moved here to Berringden, because Geoff's family were living here. Then he was posted to Northern Ireland during the Troubles, and I stayed here with the children. He was killed in Belfast, so I was a widow once again. I had lost two husbands to violent deaths, and I was still only twenty. Then I married a neighbour, Ian, he was originally from Ireland, as it happened, but he had lived in Berringden for many years. Unfortunately, he developed heart trouble and died only a couple of years after we married; at the time, I was expecting again, so my youngest daughter was born after he died.

We had always been to visit Cyprus every summer in the school holidays, and my family said I might as well stay there, now I was a widow once again, so I rented out my house in Berringden and took the children to Limassol to live. I met an older man who was Lebanese, he had a shop, and I got a job working there for him. He was a widower, so we got married; he was very kind to me and the girls, but he was killed in a car crash. His family were not very nice to me after he died, there was a dispute about the property, and they were claiming it was theirs; so we came back again to Berringden, where I still had my house, and I've been here ever since. But now the children are all grown up, and two of them are living in Cyprus, so of course, I want to be near my grandchildren. Naturally, I shall miss my youngest, she lives in Todmorden, with her husband; but I am so looking forward to the sunshine!

Chapter 19

Jess and Mash were nearing the end of their afternoon saunter through the woods when they heard a familiar cry coming from the bushes nearby. It was the bleating of Dolly the pet sheep, who belonged to the neighbours, but who was had recently fallen into the habit of escaping from their garden in search of fresh fields and pastures new…Mash and Dolly were delighted to see each other, and touched noses. Mash barked ecstatically while Dolly bleated with joy. However, Jess was worried that Dolly might find her way down to where the path through the woods reached the busy road. Luckily, Dolly always wore a dog collar, so Jess removed Mash's lead and attached it to Dolly's collar. Dolly trotted obediently beside Jess, as they made their way back to her enclosure, with Mash capering alongside. As luck would have it, there had been an end of term party at the local school, and many of the children were being collected by their parents just as the odd little trio of dog, sheep and harassed woman was passing. Jess was obliged to endure lots of jokes and comments about Mary having a little lamb which followed her to school one day, and Little Bo-Peep. Mash of course, immediately smelled the party food, and taking her opportunity while off the lead, rushed up the school steps and into the foyer. She was quickly evicted by the caretaker, who shooed her back down the steps with his broom; Jess had been unable to give chase because she was s till holding Dolly's lead. Eventually they reached Dolly's enclosure, where the anxious neighbour was searching for his lost sheep. Jess opened the gate and pushed her woolly charge inside. The neighbour said he did not see how or where she was getting out; he thought he had made the enclosure sheep-proof, but Dolly was evidently much cleverer than she appeared. As Jess and Mash turned to go home, Dolly promptly marched up a flight of overgrown steep stone steps and disappeared into the neighbour's herbaceous border.

"So that's how she's doing it! She's going up the steps! Well, I had no idea she could climb up there –or that she would want to! It's a wonder she hasn't slipped and broken something. I'll have to block those steps."
With this, the neighbour hurried off to rescue the plants in his wife's prized flowerbed, while Jess and Mash went home for tea. Jess had been planning to cook a lamb chop, but after her encounter with Dolly she decided against it and defrosted one of Alex's remaining skipped pizzas instead.
Jess's next job was to tidy up the house before Tom's visit. He was coming up from Bristol for a short break; on several previous occasions, he had complained about the state of his mother's house, which in his opinion was too cluttered and smelled of dog. Tom's first action on entering Jess's house was always to fling wide all the windows, and then to start hiding things in cupboards, usually on the topmost shelves, so that Jess did not know what had become of them, and Alex would grumble that there was no peanut butter, since it was not in its usual place by the toaster. When Jess ventured once to remark that Tom's shared house was not always especially

tidy, Tom had replied virtuously that he had spring-cleaned only last week. With this in mind, Jess planned that they should spend most of the time that Tom was visiting away from the house which so offended his sensibilities.

On his arrival, after having opened all the windows, Tom suggested a walk and a pub meal, which suited Jess fine. She immediately re-closed all the windows, since it would be unwise to leave the house open to intruders.

"This place still smells of dog!" groaned Tom. "You're so used to it, you don't realise how much it stinks. It permeates the whole house!"

Jess had always considered that a certain level of doggy smells was a small price to pay for Mash's loyal and long-lasting canine companionship. But she did not feel like getting into an argument Tom so soon after his arrival.

They walked along the canal towpath to the pub, and sat outside with their drinks enjoying the evening air. Tom went into the bar to fetch the food menu, while Jess admired the dog under the next table. It appeared to be some sort of Staffie cross, although not as pretty as Mash of course. Mash had not joined the expedition to the pub, since she had been barred from this particular establishment as a result of a dispute with another dog over a dropped chip, on a previous visit. Jess could not help overhearing snatches of the conversation between the dog-owner and his friend; it apparently centred on the best way of removing a certain type of worm from the human body – the advice given was to entice it out with the smell of bacon and wrap its head around a pencil, then pull gently. Jess shuddered. Just then, Tom reappeared with the menu and the list of specials, and asked her what she fancied eating. Jess was obliged to reply that she did not feel particularly hungry at that moment. Luckily, the two young men and the dog left just then, and Jess resolutely put all thoughts of worms and pencils from her mind. She ordered chicken in cider sauce, while Tom chose the nut roast. Tom then went on to tell her about the sit-com he was writing, set on a caravan site, and Jess ventured to offer some suggestions for future episodes. The food arrived promptly, it was delicious, and so the evening passed very pleasantly.

On their return home, they found Alex, who had been out stewarding at a football match when Tom arrived. Alex's first aid skills were frequently in demand at rock festivals and sports events, which meant he got free entry.

Having checked the weather forecast, Jess proposed an outing to Beamsley Beacon and Stump Cross caverns for the following day. Apparently it was going to be bright in the morning when they would be going up the Beacon, with rain coming in from the West during the afternoon, when it would not really matter, since by then they would be safely in the caves.

Jess recalled a previous occasion, years before, when she had visited Stump Cross Caverns. It was during her teaching days, on a field trip to the Dales. The weather had been uncertain at Bolton Abbey, turning to sleet as the children ate a soggy picnic beside the Strid. Jess did not think it was fit for the trip to continue with the riverside walk as planned; what if one of the children slipped on the mossy stones and fell into the Wharfe? The teacher leading the party agreed, but wondered what else they could find to do. Jess promptly suggested a visit to the caves, which would get them all out of the deteriorating weather, but there was a snag, namely the entry fee, as the other teacher confessed that he did not have any money on him. Jess rummaged in her purse and discovered that she had her milk money, since she had missed the milkman the previous week; however this would not be sufficient for an entire class of eleven year-olds. There was no help for it but to have a whip-round. The children were all asked to give up their ice-cream money, with the promise that it would be repaid from the school fund the following day. This they did with surprising willingness, one girl exclaiming cheerfully that it was too cold for ice-cream anyway. Another boy had broken school rules by bringing a considerable sum, enough for ice-creams all round (and more than sufficient to pay Jess's milk bill for weeks). The teachers chose to overlook this infringement of the school field trip regulations in the light of the present emergency, and they had all enjoyed their trip to the caves.

"Mum, you've told us this story before," sighed Tom, so Jess fell quiet. She checked online and made sure she had enough money for the fee.

After the excursion to the Dales, Tom offered to cook supper. Did Jess have any couscous? While Jess was rummaging in the back of the cupboard, Tom announced that he had put in an offer for a two bed-roomed house, which needed a certain amount of work doing, so the offer was fairly low, and Tom was not sure whether it would be accepted. Tom wanted a house with a garden, since he planned to grow his own vegetables, and it was while he had been inspecting the back garden that a neighbour had popped her head over the fence, anxious to tell him the story of the house and how the previous occupant had met a sad end. It turned out that the tenant had been violently murdered in the kitchen by his schizophrenic landlord. Tom had noticed that the wallpaper had been stripped off in the kitchen. The owner had subsequently been detained under the Mental Health Act and so was no longer in a position to keep up the mortgage repayments. Jess wondered what the agent had made of the telling of the tale, which was unlikely to encourage offers from prospective buyers of a squeamish disposition. Tom said the agent had been elsewhere at the time, checking the pipe-work and so had been unable to prevent him from learning about the house's recent turbulent history.

"Would you mind living there, knowing what you do about it?" asked Jess.

"It wouldn't really trouble me; after all, lots of people live in houses where someone has been murdered, they must do, or else all the homes where a murder had taken place would have to be demolished or sealed up."

"I suppose you could always get the place exorcised if there were any unsettling experiences, ghosts or poltergeists and so forth," said Jess.

"Mum, I haven't even had the offer accepted yet," sighed Tom. "Now, where do you keep the balsamic vinegar – I assume you do have some."

"Um, cider vinegar, wine vinegar and plain malt – sorry, no balsamic."

"Oh well, pass me the cider vinegar, we'll have to make do with that."

"I'm sure it will be delicious," smiled Jess. Tom's dishes generally were.

Chapter 20

I'm Nell- the resident from Hell! That's what I heard one of the carers call me, when she thought I couldn't hear her. I'm 99, getting my telegram next year if I can hang on long enough. You're the lady with the dog, aren't you? I used to have a Staffy - can you bring her up here for me to see? I don't think I can make it down to the conservatory, not with these legs. Never mind what the carers say, we pay an enormous amount of money to stay here, so we should have more say in what goes on. I know all about the residents' committee but I was thrown off it for speaking my mind. I'll let you into a secret - I don't take my tablets, I hide them in my mouth and spit them out when the carers have gone. They're all buried in that flowerpot over by the window- don't tell anyone! I wonder about the poor plant sometimes, but it seems to be holding its own. That's why I'm so outspoken, this is the real 'me', not a drugged zombie. I bet you can't get much sense from some of the resident, they're all so muddled and befuddled. But I've still got my marbles!

I ran a pub with my hubby Joe, we had it for forty-one years. That was when people used to come out to the pub all the time, not sit at home with their videos and canned beer. It was the heart and soul of the village. It's closed now, so is the village shop and the post office and the school. There's nothing there now, except an artist's studio; Otherwise - nothing, no reason to go to the place. Even the church has been demolished, they said there was subsidence and it was becoming unsafe. But now they're building two luxury houses on the site of the church, so won't those houses be affected by the subsidence, too? Or was it all a big con? I'm a bit of a sceptic, you would be too if you'd run a pub for all those years,
Now they are threatening to send me away to the 'Willows' and I don't want to go, because the 'Willows' is a secure unit for psychiatric patients. I don't know if they can do this, or whether they are using the threat to get me to behave. Can I be moved against my will? You don't know... Advocacy group - you say there might be one locally. MIND! Yes, I've heard of them, I'll give them a call. I never had any children, so no help there, although from what I've seen of others in this place, most peoples' children just want to offload you. Of course, others are very helpful and caring, but some people in here have families away in Canada or New Zealand or South Africa or America, so they're no help at all. I do try to go down and join in the activities, when I'm well enough, I like the singing and the crafts. But last week I threw some glue over silly old Edna, I couldn't help myself, because she was talking such nonsense, and now the craft group won't have me any more. They had such a job getting the glue out of her cardigan, apparently. Then, in the community singing, I accidentally sang a rude word, I was thinking about how the song went when we used to sing it back in the days when we ran the pub; but that prim and proper Mabel said she was offended and complained. The carers made out they were shocked, but I don't think their language is any too choice at times - you see, my window is above the doorway where they go out for a smoke, and I can hear what

they are saying when the window is open. There's nothing wrong with my hearing! Of course, some of those Filipina carers don't know our language very well, it was just my bad luck that they weren't on duty that day, they wouldn't have understood. It would have been my word against Mabel's, and I would have prevailed, you can be quite certain of that! Well, it's been nice talking with you - be sure to bring your dog next time. I'll be waiting!

Chapter 21

Jess and her friend Frank were on their way to a ceilidh, to be held in a tent in a sloping meadow as part of an environmental awareness festival. There was to be a vegan curry supper. They arrived early to find that preparations were still under way. Straw bales were being brought into the tent and arranged around the edge for people to use as seats. Jess looked doubtfully at the camber of the improvised floor, composed of wooden blocks which did not always properly align with one other, and wished that she was wearing more suitable shoes, maybe ones with crampons. Frank meanwhile was searching for the toilets and discovered they were back down the lane.

"Wish we had brought a torch," said Frank on his return. "It's getting quite dark, and there's not much light along the path."

The band struck up a folk tune, and the caller announced the first dance, which he claimed was an easy one to begin with. Would the dancers please arrange themselves in a Sicilian Circle. Unfortunately, he kept instructing the dancers to take hold of their partner when he meant the person opposite, creating confusion all round. Some experienced dancers knew what was expected but others were novices who had come simply to support a charity and did not have the least idea. The evening was descending into chaos, and it was not yet nine o'clock. To add to the general confusion an additional hazard presented itself, as tiny children kept rushing onto the dance-floor to find their parents, thus putting themselves in danger of being trodden on or knocked over by the whirling dancers. Jess was terrified that she would hurt a stray toddler as she concentrated on her steps. Usually there was a weary grandparent in pursuit, and once a large black dog appeared on the dance-floor. Jess supposed it must be similar to Nana, the dog who looked after the children in Peter Pan, trying to round up its charges. It was hard going dancing up the slope, and even harder trying not to slide back down towards the band. At one point, Jess almost fell into the arms of the fiddler,

Jess cursing the uneven floor, made slippery with loose straw, and the fiddler cursing Jess...

The interval was arranged early when the sound system failed, the caller explaining that he was suffering with a sore throat, so could not really carry on until the microphone had been fixed. During the interval Frank found a broom and swept the floor, while Jess was alarmed to discover a fire-juggler performing just outside the tent – and with all that straw about! She was afraid he might drop a flaming baton and set fire to the entire field. Luckily, he was an extremely accomplished performer. Next there was a commotion outside the food tent, where a lady was frantically searching for her spectacles. She had inadvertently dropped them into a heap of straw. Jess joined in the search, using her mobile phone to provide a little light. Suddenly the black dog reappeared with the glasses in its mouth. Everyone shouted with relief, but the dog, seemingly alarmed by the noise, rushed off to a far corner of the field still carrying the spectacles. A gaggle of children ran after it, calling and trying to entice it back, but it went and hid under a dark hedge. Jess could hear sheep bleating in the next field; the ceilidh and all its attendant noise must be disturbing their peace.

Eventually the dahl supper was served, the spectacles retrieved, over-excited children reunited with their parents, the dog rounded up, and the fire-juggler ushered away. Someone handy had repaired the sound system, and the band was striking up for a strip-the-willow, but Frank and Jess had had enough, and decided to return home.

"We're getting too old for all this excitement," observed Frank. "I like things to be well-organised."

"I never thought I'd say this, but I like events which pay a modicum of attention to health and safety," said Jess. "All that straw everywhere! And those kids dashing in and out of the dancing; and that fire juggler!"

"Yes, better put that one down to experience, how not to run a ceilidh."

Jess recounted the evening's events to Alex, who said that it sounded much more exciting than his Saturday night, he'd simply gone out and got pissed, and please would she let him know when they were planning to hold the next ceilidh so that he could come along and join in the fun...

Chapter 22

Jess, I want to tell you about my wife, because she can't speak to you herself. You see, she has Huntington's Chorea, one of the cruellest diseases imaginable. That famous singer, Woody Guthrie, he had it. It robs you of all control of your body and there's no cure. It's inherited, and if one of your parents has it, you've a 50% chance of developing it – it all depends on your genes. Nowadays they can test your DNA, but there was nothing like that when my wife was younger, you just had to wait and see if you got it. It was hanging over your head all the time. Well, she got to her forties and she was all right, so we thought she was safe, but then she started showing symptoms quite late. Before she was ill, we did everything together - hiking, cycling, canoeing, youth hostelling, climbing, caving – you name it, we did it. But we never had children, we thought the risk was too great. We were sad about that of course; but as things turned out, it was for the best. I worked at the mill, and she worked in the office there until she got too ill to cope. Huntington's plays havoc with your typing speeds; I hope you don't think that's an inappropriate joke, because my wife actually said it herself. Even though she knew what she was in for, she still managed to maintain a sense of humour until quite late on.

I know my wife would have wanted me to talk to you, because she thought there was far too much ignorance about Huntington's. She could not stop the shaking, and her speech was slurred, so that people who did not know about her illness thought she was drunk. They used to stare at her openly in the street. I felt like shouting at them –that she couldn't help it, it wasn't what they imagined. The disease got worse, as it inevitably does, and she eventually lost the power of speech, she could only make strange sounds; but we still went on our outings, to gardens and places of interest and such-like, because I thought the change of scene would do her good. I always believed that I could understand what she meant by her sounds, because we'd been together for such a long time. But then I got a nice woman, Jean, one of the neighbours, to come with us, to take my wife into the ladies toilet, and to see to her clothes; and I never really knew what my wife thought about this. I'd hoped she would understand that Jean was coming along to help; but now I'm afraid that she might have thought I'd got another woman lined up for after she'd gone. In the old days, she would never have suspected me - I never gave her any grounds whatever for suspicion, never; but as her mind was deteriorating, who knows what she was thinking....

Finally, she got too much for me, even with Jean's help; she needed twenty-four hour care, and she was running us ragged. So I was advised to bring her here, and put her in the high dependency unit downstairs. She would have known how it was going to end up, because she had been though it all with her own father. She had nursed him at home until finally he went into hospital, right at the end. I still come in to see her every day, but I'm sorry to say, it won't be for much longer now. Although, maybe that's for the best; you wouldn't let a dog suffer the way my wife has. Oh, I haven't told you her name, have I? They call her Grace – my Gracie.

Chapter 23

Jess was just leaving the local care home after speaking with Gracie's husband when she bumped into Anna from the Befriending scheme, whom Jess knew from church. Anna was looking rather harassed.

"I've just been to see May and she's in one of her really awkward moods," sighed Anna. "She wants me to buy her some new nightdresses, but they must be long-sleeved, high-necked and down to the floor, blue or pink floral winceyette. I ask you, where am I going to get winceyette in June?"

"I'm surprised that May is still here!" exclaimed Jess. "She told me she would be moving out in the Spring, when John returned from Australia."

"She's not really well enough to leave," said Anna." John's been causing a lot of trouble for the care home manager. I'm surprised you haven't heard."

"Oh, I simply come in to collect life stories, I'm not privy to all the gossip."

"Jess, have you got time for a coffee? I'll tell you what's been going on."

Anna led Jess to a small café around the corner from the care home, and sank wearily into one of the leather sofas. The waitress came, and they ordered cappuccinos.

"The thing is, May is completely besotted with John, and won't hear a word against him, even though she's old enough to be his mother - possibly even his grandmother! She's actually forty-odd years older than him. So it makes it difficult to befriend her, because I, and everyone else for that matter, can see she's being taken for a ride, although she won't admit it to anyone, especially not to herself, and she won't hear a word against him. She doesn't even believe John himself when he tells her he has two illegitimate children, you may know them - Imogen's twin boys, Alfie and Archie."

"Imogen who works in the Housing Office? Yes, I know her from when I was working at the Advice Centre, we used to refer homeless clients to her. I went to a New Year's Eve party at her house some years ago. But she once told me the twins' father was Jack someone or other..."

"Yes, Imogen always calls him Jack, and May knows him as John, but he's the same man. He brought the boys to visit her once, they're lovely kids, they even look quite like him, but she still would not have it that they were his children, born to an unmarried woman. She's completely deluded. Anyway, now John has full power of attorney, he collects all her pensions and the higher rate attendance allowance. She's got some form of cancer, although she won't accept the diagnosis and thinks she will be going back to John's cottage when she gets better. John of course plays along. If she's asleep when he visits he goes off to the day-room and conducts his business on a lap-top, or else he chats to the other residents, and sometimes takes them into the garden in a wheelchair; they think he's perfectly charming, which of course he can be. He got one old dear to agree to buy one of his maps, for which he charged her £60. That's his so-called business now, photo- copying old Ordnance Survey maps of the local area and staining them with tea to make them look more interesting, then framing them and selling them to people who live in that locality. Luckily, this lady had no money on her, and when she asked her son to pay for it, he was so furious he complained to the care home manager about John exploiting vulnerable older people. The management asked John to stop conducting his business in the home, but they can't ban him from visiting, because he's listed as May's next of kin. And the care workers think he's wonderful, he serenades them when he leaves in the evening, wearing his Scottish Country Dancing kilt, which actually does rather suit him, and how well he knows it..."

"And are her sons still not in the picture?" asked Jess.

"No, apparently she won't have them near. She can be so cantankerous, I'm sure I would have fallen out with her myself if she had been my mother.

And now she tells me that John is bringing a solicitor to the home next week so she can make a new will, leaving everything to him."

"There can't be much left, can there!? Surely he's spent most of it already."

"Well, the stash of money that was found up on the moors was returned after she dropped the charges against him, and that was quite a tidy sum."

"If John controls all the finances, why are you having to buy her nighties?"

"Oh, John is such a high-powered businessman, he couldn't possibly be troubled with trivial things like that! Or so she says. She thinks she will need warmer nightdresses when she goes home to the cottage. I just hope I get the money back for them, she hasn't got a penny piece in her purse."

"Why do you still do it? Surely there are easier people to befriend?"

"Well, no-one else in the scheme wants to take her on, and everyone feels that it's important that May has someone else other than John, someone independent; they want me to keep my eyes and ears open...She's really difficult, though, she's sacked me a couple of times, told me not to visit again, which was actually quite a relief, but then she's phoned the office and asked me to come back. Once it was because she wanted me to wash her delicates, but I refused, that's not what the befriending scheme is for. The home staff can do her laundry. This time it's because of the nighties." Anna paused and drank her coffee. "I never thought befriending would involve so much when I volunteered for the scheme. It can be exhausting."

"I take my hat off to you," said Jess. "You volunteers are the epitome of the Big Society." Having drunk their coffee, the women returned to the care home. As they reached the car-park, Anna suddenly clutched Jess's arm.

"Look, there he is! That's John over there, by the Land Rover. I'll ask him for some money for these wretched nighties. He can jolly well pay up."

Jess watched Anna run over to where a tall dark man in a kilt was locking his vehicle. She saw him shaking his head, and then saw Anna standing in front of him, arms akimbo, blocking his path. John returned to the Land

Rover and reached inside to find a chequebook. He wrote Anna a cheque and handed it to her with a flourish. It was Anna's turn to shake her head.

"Cash please, or I'm afraid I won't be able to get the nightclothes for May."

John must then have realised that he was dealing with that most determined of creatures, an exasperated volunteer. He went back to the car and fished about in the glove compartment, producing a handful of loose change.

"That's my parking money gone! If I get a ticket, I'll know who to blame." But this was said with a smile, since John was always charming to women.

Chapter 24

I always thought I should write my life story, but I never managed to do it, so I'll tell you instead. That's the next best thing – or better, even, as I won't have to do any of the work!

My name is Florence – they call me Florrie – and my husband is Stewart. We haven't been married long, only three years come September. We actually fell in love when we were young - we were teenage sweethearts - but they wouldn't let us marry, in fact, it was against the law for us to marry. You see, we were first cousins, and cousin marriage was not allowed back then, because of the risk of inherited medical conditions; if both husband and wife have the same grandparents, then it's more likely that any inherited conditions will have a chance to surface and lead to congenital illnesses.

So unfortunately, we had to part, and we both ended up marrying other people. Stewart had a family, a son and two daughters, while I trained to be a nurse; eventually I became a Sister at the new Stroke Unit in Berringden. I did not marry until after I was qualified. You see, it had taken me a good while to get over not being allowed to marry Stewart, so I threw myself into my training and work. My husband was the administrator at the Stroke unit.

Eventually, Peter, my husband died, and so did Stewart's wife. We had not kept in touch, so it was quite a surprise when we both found ourselves at a club for the bereaved. A shock, really, but in a nice way. Imagine finding your first sweetheart again after all those years! Of course, this time there was no reason why we shouldn't get together; the law forbidding first cousin marriage had been abolished, and I was too old to have children so we had no worries about inherited disease. But, coming from a nursing background, I think that law was sensible. Our neighbours are first cousins, and their son is not well, he has an inherited condition, it's hard to see him suffering, poor little thing. And his life expectancy is not good.

Stewart and I were very happy for a couple of years, but then Stewart began forgetting things, he would leave the door unlocked and windows wide open and so forth. He couldn't remember if we'd had tea, or what day it was. Because I'd been a nurse, I realised that his short-term memory was failing, and that it was likely due to TIAs - mini-strokes, tiny bleeds in the brain. It's a form of dementia; not Alzheimer's, which is more of a gradual deterioration, but a step-wise decline, with a bit more function being lost after each small stroke. He's still a lovely man, and I'm so glad we found each other after all those years, but he's not the Stewart I fell for at sixteen. His personality will alter as the disease progresses, and no-one can do anything about it. It's such a cruel illness.

I brought him in here because he was becoming too much for me, I'm 80, you know! It was becoming a struggle to get him to do anything, even putting his clothes on was a battle. But the carers here are very good, they're young and strong and the chivvy him along in a good-natured way, and he responds to them. His family are wonderful, they accepted me as their step-mother at once, although they were still mourning the loss of their mother. So even though I had no children of my own, at least I have a good step-family to support me. I know I shall need it!

Chapter 25

"I'm off to Glastonbury tomorrow," said Alex. "Doing some stewarding. Lots of my friends going as well - gonna be great! Great line-up! You ought to come one year, Mum, you could hang out in the Healing Field...you've never been to a rock festival, have you, just those folkie ones..."

"I have been to a pop festival, as it happens, but it was a long time ago. 1970, at Krumlin."

"Krumlin? That's not very far from here is it? Up on the tops near the M62? You're having me on, surely there's never been a festival there..."

"Oh yes there was! I went to it, but only for the afternoon, because it was washed out by a torrential downpour, even though it was held in the middle of summer. It was my first year at Leeds, and I came out in an old car with a civil engineer who wanted to look at the new motorway bridge. We were intending to camp, but conditions were so awful that we went back that evening. The only act I heard was Fairport Convention, but if I had been there on the Friday I would have heard Elton John, and also an act called the Humblebums, who turned out to be Billy Connolly and Gerry Rafferty. They were not at all well known at the time. I actually wanted to hear the Kinks, they were scheduled to play on the Saturday, but they never arrived. There were problems with the festival finances as well as the dreadful weather, and I think one of the organisers absconded. In the end, it was a complete mud-bath, and the people who had stayed the night had to be rescued by the Civil Defence, they made up gallons of hot soup to revive everyone, because they were in danger of getting hypothermia. Some had to be taken to hospital. It's all on the web, if you want to read about it. The strange thing was that Nick was also up there, but I did not know him at the time, we did not meet until I moved here to Berringden, years later."

"Doesn't sound like it was a lot of fun. Let's hope we have better weather this weekend in Somerset! Though it often is very wet for Glasto, a lad I know got trench foot one year..."

"Well, good luck; I'll be happy simply to watch in on television," said Jess. "Although it's really not the same these days, without John Peel..."

" John Peel - didn't you once meet him at some tea-party?"

"Yes, I bumped into him at a charity garden-party near Stowmarket, he was a patron of the charity, and I didn't know anyone there apart from Frank."

Jess recalled the occasion, many years before, when Frank had asked her to accompany him to this event, organised by a mental health charity for which he had once worked. Frank did not wish to go alone, as he considered that this would look 'sad', when the invitation said to bring a guest. Of course, as soon as they had arrived, lots of people recognised

Frank and whisked him away to meet other former colleagues, leaving Jess quite alone. Then she had spied a familiar-looking figure arriving, in the shape of the radio presenter John Peel. The chairman greeted him with a cup of tea, but was then called away, leaving John on his own with his teacup. Jess was similarly nursing hers, so went across.

"Have you got a minute, John?"

"Yes, of course, come and sit down!" In no time at all they were chatting away like old friends, since both had teenage children at the time and were coping with similar problems arising from adolescent behaviour. Jess was a keen listener to John's "Home Truths" radio programme, on which her brother Jeff had once appeared, recounting an odd episode from the time of the Investiture of Prince Charles in 1969, when Jeff had camped beneath a trestle table in the centre of Caernarfon. There was a cloth draped over it, so Jeff had been able to make himself quite cosy. He awoke to the sound of a military voice explaining the top-secret security arrangements for the day. Jeff had held his breath, but luckily, no-one had bothered to check whether there was anyone camping under the table, so he remained undiscovered. John Peel recalled Jeff's appearance on Home Truths, and he had also heard of Hebden Bridge, since his wife was from Yorkshire, so there was plenty to talk about, and they were happily engaged in conversation twenty minutes later when Frank eventually returned to look for Jess.

Jess's next engagement was to attend the graduation ceremony of her friend Sehlile. Assisted by Jess, who had gladly paid the airfare in order to secure her friend's safety, Sehlile had fled a dangerous situation in Zimbabwe bringing nothing with her apart from a small bag of clothes. In the intervening years and now a British citizen, she had married, had a baby daughter, worked as a travel consultant, published newspaper articles, and studied for her degree. Jess was very proud of her friend.

The ceremony was presided over by Imran Khan, who had exchanged his cricketing whites for the splendour of the university Chancellor's robes. Jess though back to her own graduation, many years before; she had felt unable to attend the conferment ceremony, coming so soon after the death of her mother. Everyone else had proud parents in attendance, and Jess simply could not face the day in her newly orphaned state. Later, when the time had come for Jess's Masters Degree conferment, she had been away in

Botswana. Jess had of course attended Tom's degree ceremony in Bristol cathedral but was surprised at how different this present ceremony was. Some of the new graduates behaved as though they were contestants in a reality television show, posing on stage in the manner of celebrities, while their friends shrieked and whistled and cheered wildly. Jess thought this was rather inappropriate, but reflected that it appeared to be symptomatic of the times, with everyone encouraged to snatch their fifteen seconds of fame. Attention spans were now so short that Andy Warhol's allocation of fifteen minutes seemed a generous allowance. When Sehlile came to receive her scroll, Jess was pleased that the audience appreciation was confined to polite applause, rather than the earlier raucous behaviour.

Chapter 26

My name is Mywfanwy, and I was born in 1922. My father had moved from South Wales when work was hard to find, that's why I have a Welsh name but a London accent! We actually spoke Welsh at home because my father disliked having to speak English; I think he was quite homesick. I was always musical, and I leaned to play the violin and the accordion, so I was in great demand for dances and community sing-songs - there was more community spirit about then. Of course, it was the Depression, and times were hard, so we had to make our own entertainment. Then the War broke out, and I became an auxiliary WAF and worked at the airport; I was one of those girls you see in the old black and white films, moving the planes around on charts. I met my husband during the war, and we married as soon it ended. Our son, Laurie, was born in 1949, and I was told that because of damage during the birth, it would be dangerous for me to have another baby. My husband got a job at Victoria Station, he worked hard, and eventually he rose to become chief cashier. I had a variety of jobs – you could leave one job on Friday and start another on Monday morning, there were plenty going. You could go where the wages were higher, or the conditions were better, or the people were nicer, whatever you wanted. So I worked in a factory, then a shop, then an office, and my wages helped us to save up for a house. Lots of women did not work in those days, sometimes this was because their husbands wouldn't let them, they thought they should be at home all the time; but mine never stood in my way like that, and of course, it made all the difference to our savings. My dad was living with us, he looked after Laurie when he came home from school, so Welsh is his first language as well.

My husband could be a difficult man, and anyway, he had two left feet, so he refused to come dancing with me, and I would take Laurie. He learned to quickstep, waltz, and foxtrot and he was only eleven! He grumbled about having to come with me, but had to do as he was told. Children did, then; there was none of this answering back My husband and Laurie had some right royal battles when Laurie was growing up. He wanted Laurie to take a secure Civil Service job, but Laurie wanted to go to Art School. My husband made him leave school and go out to work, but after a year, Laurie packed the job in and announced that he was going to college. My husband was furious, and threw Laurie out of the house. The poor lad had nowhere to go, so he lived rough for over a year. He used to do odd jobs on farms, and eat wild food like pigeons that he caught with a catapult. He was living as a tramp, and I only heard from him occasionally, when he had a few spare coppers for the phone. I should have done more to stand up to my husband, but I doubt it would have made much difference. Anyway, as the second winter drew on, Laurie just walked back in one day, and my husband did not say anything; secretly, he was ashamed of what he had done, throwing his only son out onto the street.. After that, he had the sense to just let Laurie get on with his life, but the two of them barely spoke. I was stuck in the middle, and it was not an easy position to be in.

When my husband retired, he wanted to leave Croydon and come back to Yorkshire, where his family was from originally, so we moved here. It was so much cheaper to live here, and we could finally afford to buy a house, because the Coal Board was selling their stock off at the time. I've been here ever since, although I've never really settled. And now my husband's gone, and I'm a widow, I really miss Croydon, although I know I'll never be able to go back. The property prices down there are double what they are here... Laurie hates it here, although he has made the best of it, joining all sorts of clubs and organisations. But he can't seem to get anything more than temporary jobs, it's difficult nowaday, like the Depression all over again now the pits have all closed. I was afraid Social Services might make me sell my house when I came in here, they do if they can, because it saves them having to pay care fees. When my husband died, I put his half of the house in Laurie's name, so that I only own half, and who would want to buy half an ex-Coal Board house? And the transfer happened more than seven years ago, so they can't touch us; and they'd have a job getting Laurie out of his half of the house, they'd have to go to court to do it. After all, an Englishman's house is his castle! And a Welshman's!

Chapter 27

Jess and her neighbour Mark were making one of their occasional trips to the local tip with a large number of bags which mostly contained clippings from a privet hedge. Mark was very environmentally aware, using public transport or riding his bike; but since the council did not collect garden waste, he was glad of the use of Jess's Micra when the occasion demanded. The tip was the other side of Hebden Bridge, and Jess had filled the car boot with a piece of old carpet and some bits of wood she had found in the shed. She had offered the wood to another neighbour with a wood-burning stove, but he had declined, because it had been treated and would give off noxious fumes when burnt. Jess pulled up beside the garden waste skip and Mark emptied his hedge clippings. The final bag contained some rubble from his cellar, so they went to find the skip for that. Peering into it, Jess was astonished to see a number of china items, seemingly in perfectly sound condition. She tried to pick out the items, but they were just out of her reach.

"Mark, just look at those plates, they don't appear to be chipped! And that jug is really pretty. I can't understand people throwing away good stuff when charity shops are always appealing for bric-a-brac."

Mark sighed, as he could see where this was leading. "I suppose you'd like me to climb in and rescue the china before I put my rubble in."

"Oh, would you? I can take it to a charity shop - or even use it myself. The next lot of rubble in there will smash it all so it won't be any use."

Mark sighed in a resigned fashion and climbed down into the half-full skip. He handed several intact pieces of the china up to Jess, who put them carefully into a spare plastic bag. Just as Mark was climbing out again, one of the tip attendants came over and began shouting at him.

"Hey, come out, you're not supposed to be in there! It's against Health and Safety! We can only go in if we're wearing hard hats and heavy boots."

Mark was wearing trainers, and was bareheaded so Jess apologised. "I'm sorry, I asked him to go in, it seemed such a shame for all this lovely china to be broken when someone could make use of it."

The attendant glowered at her. "You're supposed to be putting stuff in, not taking things out. Technically it's stealing from the council."

Jess opened her plastic bag and showed the attendant the china Mark had retrieved. "It's all in a good cause, I'll send it to charity.".Mark, meanwhile, had emerged from the skip and was dusting himself down.

The attendant peered into Jess's bag. "Eh up, love, I see what you mean, there's some right good stuff in there. My mum collects bits and bats of china, she always says to look at the maker's mark on the bottom. This one says Alfred Meakin, and here's a bit of Crown Derby! Now which charity shop would you be thinking of taking it to? There's that new one in aid of the greyhound rescue place just opened up near the market. I could turn a blind eye if you said it was going there."

Jess nodded, the attendant smiled, and Mark heaved a sigh of relief. The attendant, who seemed now to regard them as new- found friends, was rummaging in an adjacent skip, and emerged with an ironing board.

"This any good to you, love? In perfect condition, not a mark on it, just needs a new cover." Jess, who hated ironing and did as little of it as possible, was about to decline the attendant's kind offer, when Mark spoke up, saying that he might well be able to make use of it. The ironing board joined the bag of china in the car boot. It seemed that they would be taking away from the tip almost as much as they had brought. They made their way back to Hebden Bridge. Mark went to buy some brown rice, while Jess made a beeline for the greyhound charity shop, where the rescued china was gratefully received. Jess knew that the greyhound industry often destroyed dogs whose running careers were over, and the TIA charity rescued as many as possible. They had a farm up on the moors above the Berringden Valley where the dogs could live out their lives in peace and safety, with the possibility of adoption -a cause after Jess's heart.

Chapter 28

Buongiorno, Jess, va bene? Come in and sit down! I have been thinking about what I want to tell you – shall I start now?

My name is Franco, but I'm known as Frankie in England. The first Italian you've met with a Yorkshire accent, I'll bet! I came here to Yorkshire as a prisoner of war. I was very young, and I had never been anywhere so cold! We were put to work on a farm, and it was there that I met Jennie, she was a Land Girl, and our eyes met across a field of potatoes. Of course, we were not supposed to have anything to do with the English people, but looks can say more than words – at least, we Italians can make them say more, the English are not too good at this. Jennie and I used to find ways of snatching a few moments together, when we were loading the cart, or fetching more sacks. Believe me, there will always be ways for two young people in love!

After the war, I went home to see my family, but all I could think of was returning to be with Jennie. As luck would have it, there was a labour shortage here and so I was able to come back to work in the mills. I had already learned English, so that was an advantage. Jennie had waited for me, despite opposition from her family, because of course Italy had been the enemy during the war and feelings were still running high against us 'Eye-ties' I worked hard, and we married when she was twenty-one. We bought a house, and raised a family, three boys, Carlo, Marco and Franco.

Then I heard of a small company taking people on coach holidays across Europe to Italy, and they needed an Italian speaker to escort the trips. I volunteered, so we were able to travel for free to many different parts of Italy, and the boys could get to know my homeland. Of course, it was not all plain sailing and sometimes mishaps would occur. On one trip, a passenger broke her leg and ended up in hospital, we had to come home without her; however, I managed to find an English-speaking lady to visit her every day, she was actually the wife of the taxi-driver that took me to the hospital. Another time, one man died on the holiday, and I had to make the necessary arrangements to repatriate his body and assist his wife. Then there was the time when a woman had a nervous breakdown and required psychiatric attention; and of course, the usual things like lost passports, mislaid luggage, and unfortunately once or twice a bag snatch. English people often seem to blithely go abroad without any idea of the language of the country they are visiting, so I don't know how they would have managed in these situations if I had not been there. The Italian currency was lira then, with notes in large denominations, so it was easy to become confused with all those zeros. I was often able to stop members of our party paying more than they needed to for things such as coffee and postcards.

We went mainly to Tuscany, it was not nearly so popular then as it is now; we would stay at a hilltop village called Castellina Marittima. We visited all the usual places, Pisa, Firenze, Lucca, Siena, and also San Gimignano and Volterra. We also took other trips to the Lakes, Como, Maggiore and Garda. We went to the opera in Verona and of course we went to Venice. Once we went all the way to Sorrento, that's quite a long way South. One of the gentlemen of the party had been at Monte Cassino in the war, so we had to go there. Italy is such a varied and beautiful country, I really enjoyed showing it to others, from my adopted county of Yorkshire - which is almost as lovely! I say 'almost', because Italy has more sunshine, and you know that England can look so dreary in the rain. Jennie and I used to argue about which country was more beautiful, Italy or England! Our boys are born Yorkshire men, so I was always outvoted within our family. But I made sure they learned to speak Italian, and they always used it when they were there. I would go around the house with the boys, pointing out everything with its Italian name –, mela for apple, latte for milk etc. Now that Italian food and coffee is so popular here, people know a little more of the language. Jennie struggled with it at first, but after years of listening to me, she finally got the hang of it. And she eventually learned to cook Italian food as well, which was a pleasant surprise to me. We used to have to search for proper pasta, it was not widely available when we were first married. You had to go to a specialist deli. I must have loved Jennie very much, mustn't I, to have been willing to survive on a diet of Yorkshire pudding and pies and fish and chips and mushy peas! But I always had a special affection for potatoes, because it was in a potato field that Jennie and I first met. After Jennie died, I thought I would return to Italy, and I did live there for a year, but do you know what? After all those years here, I missed my home in Yorkshire – rain and all! Carlo and Franco are both working overseas, in America and Australia, but Marco is here in Leeds, with his wife and family, so that's where I decided to settle. Who would have thought it, eh? If it had not been for the war, and those potatoes, I would never have met my dear Jennie, my own Yorkshire lass!

Chapter 29

Jess had been given a ticket to attend a concert at the O2 arena in London as a special birthday present from her generous friend Carmel. She planned to stay with her younger brother Peter near Camberley, and travel up to London on the train. Not wanting to return to Surrey late at night, she had booked to stay overnight in Earls Court Youth Hostel.

The concert was to hear Placido Domingo and Angela Gheorghiu, with the Royal Philharmonic Orchestra., and Jess was looking forward to it very much. Some years ago, she had attended an open-air performance by Jose Carreras at Castle Howard, complete with firework finale, and she had also once been to a concert given by Luciano Pavarotti in Manchester, so she was pleased to be getting the chance at last to hear Domingo, who was her favourite of the celebrated three tenors.

The approach to the O2 was impressive, and although it was still early, thousands of people were arriving from the Tube, by bus, by taxi, and disembarking from the Thames boats. Jess bought a programme, it was rather expensive she thought, at £10. She decided there was still time to have a cup of tea, so made her way to a café. There was a queue, which was being efficiently managed, with people wanting only drinks being speedily served. A young woman brought Jess her plastic beaker of tea – no such thing as a cup these days, she reflected, and she went to find a seat. There were some spare chairs at a table, so she asked the two ladies sitting there if she could join them; they nodded pleasantly, but just as she was about to sit down Jess tripped, and spilled her tea. Luckily, it did not go over the ladies, but Jess was upset. "I was so looking forward to that drink," she sighed.

"Ask them to get you another one," urged one of the ladies. Jess doubted that she could get a fresh cup without paying, but the teabag was still in the bottom of her cup, so she explained to the young woman managing the queue what had happened, and asked if she could have fresh water for the teabag. On hearing of her plight, the young woman immediately discarded the old teabag and replaced it with a fresh one, free of charge. Jess thought she would never again complain about Starbucks and globalisation. She returned to her table, where the ladies, who introduced themselves as Mona and Marjorie, began asking her where she had come from. They were surprised to hear that Jess was also from Yorkshire – they were themselves from Leeds, and had come down on the coach. Marjorie was a Placido Domingo groupie, who had followed him all over the world to hear him sing on three continents. However, even before the main arena door were open, her chief concern at present was the fact that their coach had dropped them off some considerable distance from the entrance, and she did no relish the prospect of the long walk back after the performance.

"Her legs aren't so good these days," explained Mona. "We'll just have to hope the coach doesn't go without us. You'd think they'd know that people coming by coach wouldn't be able to walk so far."

Jess murmured sympathetically, and the discussion then moved to the forthcoming switch-over to digital television in Yorkshire, and the problems this might bring. Mona had already tried out a set-top box, but had been able to receive only broadcasts from the North-East, when she really wanted the transmissions from Emley Moor. After all, why on earth would people in Leeds want to watch Look North Newcastle, which was of no interest to them at all...She hoped things would be sorted out soon so she would be able to get the right channels. There was supposed to be some help for the over 75s in tuning their digi-boxes, so she would have to try to get a man in to do it.

"You haven't paid £10 for that programme, have you?" queried Marjorie, her tone indicating her disapproval. Jess admitted that she had, somewhat rashly bought the lavish souvenir programme, but it was, after all, a once in a lifetime occasion for her, since she did not have the resources to become an intercontinental Domingo groupie. On approaching a sales counter, the ladies had been scandalised to discover the price of the programme, and Marjorie now demanded to look at it in order to assess its value.

"It's less than twenty pages, that's over fifty pence a page! We wondered who on earth would buy them! And you say you're from Yorkshire?"

"Um, from Devon originally," said Jess, "Although I moved North many years ago," she added. The women smiled knowingly at each other.

"Well, that explains it! You're not a Yorkshire person after all, you're a Southerner! There's not a Yorkshire woman born that would part with £10 for something like that..."

Soon it was time to go in, and Jess, refreshed by the tea, bade her new friends goodbye, since their seats in the arena were on a different level to hers. She queued up to pass through the security gates, where her bag was searched and a small bottle of juice discovered. Jess had been unaware that, just as on airlines, it was not permitted to take liquids into the arena. She was informed that she had either to drink it or dispose of it. She drank it, and then immediately regretted her action, since this would necessitate another yet trip to the loo. Luckily there were plenty of toilets. Finally, Jess found her place, in the cheapest seating area, on the end of a row some distance away from the stage. As she sat down, she was greeted by the elderly woman in the next seat, who immediately embarked on an account of her life history. She had been born before the war, in Singapore, of a military family, but had been living for many years in Haywards Heath, from where she had travelled up today, much to the displeasure of her children, who did not think she should be gadding about in London at the age of 88; but as she had told them, what did it matter if an old woman was attacked on the way home, she would have heard the concert, and that was really all that mattered. Her daughter would meet her at the station. Jess had to say 'shush' at this point in the narrative, since the orchestra had finished tuning up, the conductor had arrived, and the concert was about to begin. However, the lady was nothing daunted, and when Angela Gheorghiu took to the stage, she began a running commentary on the diva's appearance.

"I'm not sure about that dress; do you think it suits her? I thought she would have chosen something more glamorous, given the occasion. It almost makes her look fat! And as for her hair; do you think she has a wig, or hair extensions? Those large screens don't do her any favours, do they – see how wrinkled she's becoming. Dear me, how old she's looking!"

Jess glanced about for a spare seat to which she could move, but there was none available. The twittering spoiled her enjoyment of Miss Gheorghiu's performance, and even when Placido came on, her neighbour did not stop.

"How marvellous he looks; you wouldn't think he'd been ill, would you? His voice sounds just as good as it did when he was in his prime. Isn't he wonderful? So handsome! I love this aria, one of his best, I should say. And now he's singing in English –'Man of La Mancha,' one of my favourites!"

Jess felt that her own impossible dream would be to escape from the unwanted commentary and be able to enjoy the rest of the concert in peace. She kept glaring at the woman, but to no avail. During the interval, Jess queued for the loo, along with every other woman in that part of the arena, and there was no time left to investigate the possibility of finding a new seat in a different block, so she was obliged to return to her original place. Angela reappeared on stage in a more glamorous frock, and with her hair arranged differently, both of which met with Jess's neighbour's approval.

"That dress is so much nicer, look at all those sequins, do you suppose they are hand-sewn? And her hair is better like that, it makes her look younger."

Jess had decided to ignore the woman throughout the second half, but she had been brought up to be polite, and she found herself agreeing that the new dress was much prettier, but adding "let's listen, now, shall we?"

At the end of the remarkable performance, seven encores were given, Angela appearing in yet another gorgeous gown, and huge bouquets were presented to the principals. It had been a memorable night, although Jess wished she could have listened to a little more of it uninterrupted. She supposed she would have to resort to YouTube when she got back home. Then it was time to join yet another enormous queue, this one was to get out of the arena and into the underground. A young woman on the Tube looked startled at the huge invasion of passengers joining the train.

"What on earth's been going on?" she asked Jess.

"An operatic concert at the O2 with Placido Domingo."

"Oh, one of the three tenors; I remember them. Did he sing that 'Nessun Dorma' football song?" asked the woman, looking at Jess's programme. Jess was pleased to report that he had not, since she considered that that particular aria had suffered from overkill since the World Cup. The late Luciano Pavarotti had sung 'Nessun Dorma' at his concert in Manchester, but tonight Placido Domingo had given lots of other wonderful stuff instead, including Otello, Die Walkure and West Side Story. It was hard to imagine a more varied selection. The woman returned Jess's programme.

"Looks lovely." Jess agreed that it had indeed been - lovely

Chapter 30

My name is Dorothy, known as Dot. I'm a bit younger then most of the other residents, as I'm only 75. I'm in here because of mobility problems, and because I'm partially deaf. Don't worry, I can lip-read, I learned how to do that years ago in the mills, because of the noise of the machinery. That's how we mill girls used to communicate, we would stand in the loom gate and simply mouth the words to one another.

I was actually born in London, but I was evacuated during the war to Harrogate –that was my introduction to Yorkshire, and I've lived here ever since. My mother and sister came with me from London, and we did not want to go back after the war, our street had been bombed out and my father had been killed in action in the Far East. So there was nothing to go back to. We settled in Bradford, and I went to work in the mills after I left school. I worked in several. In those days you could walk out of one job at lunchtime and be in another one that same afternoon. When I was twenty, I got engaged to a man who worked in the same mill as I did, but it fell through. We had decided to emigrate to Canada, and he went on ahead, the plan was that he was going to send for me when he had got a job and somewhere to live. But he was in digs at first, and he went off with the landlady's daughter! I did not know this for quite a time, he kept writing to say that things were not quite ready, and putting me off for another six months, but not telling me the real reason. Then I heard from friends that knew his family in Bradford that he had actually got married and had a baby with this Canadian woman! Goodness knows when or if he would have ever got round to telling me himself. It was such a shock! I wrote to tell him what I thought of him, I did not mince my words, 'hell hath no fury like a woman scorned'; and do you know what his reply was? No word of apology, just a scruffy little note, asking me to return the engagement ring! Needless to say, I did not! I have it still. I'll show it to you - it's on the dressing table over there. Pretty, isn't it? A diamond ....

I decided then that I had had enough of men, if that was how they behaved, and thought I would devote my life to travel. I was still living at home with my mother, and I saved up for a few years until I had enough money to go around the world. I've been travelling ever since, until last year, when I came in here. You name any country, and I'll most likely have been to it – I've even visited Antarctica. I did a cruise of the Southern Ocean in 2001.

Of course, I still had to work, but I needed long holidays, so I set up a nursery school – this was long before all these Ofsted regulations- so I could have three months holiday a year. The premises we rented for the nursery had a large plot of land which was all overgrown, so I cleared it and set up an allotment. Some of the parents were keen gardeners and so we grew the food for the children's lunches. I became interested in organic gardening, and set up a gardening club. My travels took me to Cuba, where they go in for organic gardening in a big way. Of course, it's much warmer there, and they can get three crops a year because of the longer growing season. I visited a collective farm, and went to a meeting which Castro addressed, his speech went on for hours, and I didn't understand much of it, knowing very little Spanish, but it was interesting to go. There was music and dancing and poetry, it was a wonderful occasion. I also visited an old folks' home, they were all sitting out in the sun, not like here, where the wind whips across the moors and if you try to set foot in the front garden you get blown back indoors again. They had an organic garden at the Cuban old folks' home, and that gave me the idea of setting one up here. I asked the Manager and she said I should put it to the residents' committee, and we got that plot round the corner - you'll have passed it on your way in from the car park. It's more sheltered that side. Because I'm in this wheelchair, and lots of us can't bend, some of the beds are raised and all the paths are wide enough for my chair – we got funding from the lottery to set it up. There's a sensory bed for the blind residents, with lavender and mint and suchlike. You be sure to spend a few minutes there on your way out. It's my legacy –I've no kids, but I will have left a lovely garden.

Chapter 31

Jess was becoming rather anxious about Paul and Naomi's peahen, since she was not in her usual place with the peacock on the lawn. Jess hoped that the poachers had not taken her. After searching around the garden, Jess eventually discovered her, sitting in a flowerbed in the kitchen garden, under the honeysuckle bush. The peahen was evidently broody, and appeared to be incubating eggs. Jess did not disturb her and made a mental note not to allow Mash into the kitchen garden. Just then, the peahen honked loudly and flew off to the patio, where she and her mate usually came to receive their breakfast of nuts and seeds. Jess observed five large eggs in the nest. She wondered whether the peacock had fulfilled his duty and hoped that the eggs were fertile and that there would be pea-chicks running about in due course. The peahen ate her food quickly, then returned to her nest. Since it was a fine day, Jess decided to take Mash to a nearby lake for a walk. Mash always enjoyed jumping in the water to cool off on hot days. It was a popular spot, and Mash was wagging her tail at everyone, when two little boys ran up.

"Have you seen Colin? Did he go in this direction?"

"Oh dear, how old is Colin?" asked Jess, thinking they must be referring to a missing child. "I haven't seen anyone this way."

The boys ran on ahead, shouting "Come back here, Colin!"

Jess stopped the couple walking behind the children, assuming that they were the boys' parents, and asked them for a description of the missing Colin, but the couple simply glared at her and walked by without a word. Then she saw an elderly lady struggling to keep up.

"It's their granddad who's missing, so please don't worry. He ran off to tease them - he used to be a great runner in his younger days."

How very modern, to call one's grandfather by his first name, thought Jess. With the same, excited cries of "We've found him! Colin's here!" were heard, as an elderly man came puffing around the corner.
"Really Colin," said Jess, "You shouldn't run off like that, worrying us all!" Everyone laughed, and Jess and Mash continued on their way.

A party of inebriated young men was lounging on the lake shore, tossing beer cans into the water and then throwing stones at the cans, most of which missed. Mash barked and wagged her tail, as she loved young men. One of them called out to his mates, "Hey, look that dog's well nice!" whereupon another lad staggered up to the path to stroke Mash, who immediately rolled on her back in order that he could tickle her tummy. The young man giggled, and Jess sighed.

"She really is a dreadful flirt!"

"Aw, she's well cool." Suddenly the lad's expression changed.

"Gotta go!" He rolled down the path, and was sick in a bush.

So many young people seemed to have problems relating to alcohol, these days, reflected Jess. Last Good Friday, for instance, she and her neighbour Mark had gone to Heptonstall to watch the traditional Pace Egg mummers' play. Alex and some friends had also been amongst the crowd, and they were all a bit merry, in fact one lad had passed out on the cobbles. There was also a young girl, who clearly had consumed far more than was good for her, so much so that she was now having difficulty standing up. After the play had finished, Alex asked Jess if he and a few friends could have a lift back down to Hebden Bridge, since Sonia was not feeling very well.

"What shall we do about this chap in the gutter?" asked Jess.

"Oh, we'll leave Beanie," said Alex. "He's well out of it."

Jess had agreed to take Sonia, Alex, and two of the others; Mark said he was staying longer, although Jess thought he was quite understandably wishing to distance himself from the drunkards. Her car was parked around the corner so Alex and another lad had more or less to drag Sonia the few hundred yards towards the car. Jess noted several tut-tuts and looks of disapproval from passers-by, directed, not at Sonia, but at her. People must have thought that Jess was Sonia's mother, and were wondering what sort of a woman could allow her daughter to get into that sort of state; and it was still only four o'clock in the afternoon.

Arriving back home after her trip to the lake, Jess was surprised to find a box containing an electric food mixer on the doorstep. She was puzzling as to what it might be doing there when Kate appeared.
"Ah, you're back. I left you that mixer, it doesn't actually work and of course Adrian won't fix it, he simply ordered a new one, so I thought you'd like it. You haven't got one, have you? No, I thought as much!"

"But I can't mend it either! I don't have those skills."

"Of course I realise that, but I thought one of the many men who come to your house might be able to get it going again."

"The 'many men'? You make my home sound like a house of ill repute!"

"Of course I don't mean that! I just thought there was Alex here, and doesn't Nick still come at the weekends to watch football on TV? Or maybe Tom could mend it when he comes for a visit."
.

"Neither Alex nor Nick is likely to be at all interested; it's as much as I can do to get them to take out the rubbish or the recycling; and as for Tom, he comes here for a holiday, not to mend broken-down electrical appliances..."

"Really, Jess, you're not being very constructive. It would be a complete waste to throw the mixer away, we live in such an extravagant society, squandering resources - it will be on my conscience if you won't take it."
.

Jess realised with a sigh that there was absolutely no chance of Kate taking her mixer back. Maybe she could get Mark to take a look at it; or if not, she would have to set it aside until their next sortie to the tip.

Chapter 32

Hello Jess, good to see you again. As you know, my wife and I are both in here; Emily has dementia and I have a list of ailments as long as your arm. Oh, of course, you need my name. It is Clifford, I was born in 1927, so was Emily. We simply could not manage at home, and, being in here is fine, because I have so much more time for my writing, now I don't have to do everything for my wife. I must have written getting on for a thousand letters to the press over the years, and a good many have been published. I correspond with people all over the world, mainly on environmental matters. I'm sure that toxins in the environment have contributed to my sorry state of health, and possibly caused Emily's dementia as well.

I was called up to do National Service just after the war, and sent out to Palestine. It was at the time of the civil war in the British Mandate of Palestine, when the Jews were setting up the state of Israel as their homeland. It was a bloody war, other countries were sending in troops to support the various factions, and there were casualties on all sides, including the British, but we had to leave in May 1948 when the Mandate expired. I came home and married Emily and started work as a printer.

You've no idea how different printing was in those pre-computer days – or maybe you are just old enough to remember the old way of type -setting, with racks of characters all set by hand. "Hot metal" they used to call it. I developed osteoporosis, which men can get as well as women, and I also had trouble with my prostate, and other things I won't bore you with. I began to wonder what was causing all these problems, and came to the conclusion that there were things around us which are harmful to humans. This was long before environmentalism became all the rage, and some people called me a crank, but they don't laugh at me so much now! I began a letter-writing campaign, and have never stopped. I learned a long time ago not to take criticism personally, it's just water off a duck's back to me. Just as long as it wasn't fluoridated water!

I have been involved with all the anti-war and peace protest campaigns since the Second World War, because of course I witnessed civil war at first hand in Palestine. I've been on countless demos, held hands with thousands of others to encircle the US base at Menwith Hill, up on the moors above Harrogate; Faslane, Holy Loch, Aldermaston Greenham Common, anti-Trident, Barrow-in Furness, Hyde Park, Trafalgar Square - you name it, I was there. I think I met you on one of those marches, didn't I? I can't go now of course, but I always try to send a message of support. Meanwhile Emily preferred to stay home, keeping house, doing the garden, looking after the children and then the grandchildren, and generally being busy with her various domestic duties. She's never been what you might call a firebrand but that suited us fine. We complemented each other. Now it looks like we are going in for another pointless war. First our politicians court these leaders and arm them, then they denounce them as tyrants and bomb them. Don't get me wrong, I've no love for any of these despots, but it seems to me that we have learned absolutely nothing about the Middle East since I was there in 1947. And I'm afraid we never will.

Our children felt that we would be better coming in here, now that we both have health problems, and it's rather a lovely setting, don't you think? Our biggest regret was having to give up our chickens. We kept them for years, and never had any problem with the fox, since we used to put out some food for him every night; that way, he never took our hens! Not once! Our daughter has them now, she has a big garden and the grandchildren love collecting the eggs for breakfast every morning, and of course, we visit from time to time. I'm convinced that the hens recognise us when we go!

Chapter 33

Dolly the sheep being loaded into a trailer as Jess passed by on her way to the woods with Mash. Surely she wasn't being sent for lamb chops?

"Don't worry," called the neighbours, noticing Jess's look of alarm. "We're taking her to stay with friends for a couple of weeks while we're away on holiday. They have a two acre garden, so she should enjoy herself."

"Maa" bleated Dolly, before returning to munching the hay in the trailer.

Later that day Jess caught the train to Todmorden, where there was a craft fair. She spent a few minutes browsing a leaflet about the Incredible Edible initiative, founded some years ago; this had recently received visits from such luminaries as Michael Portillo and Prince Charles. Noticing her interest, a man bounded across the room and engaged her in conversation.

"Hi, do you want to know something about our Incredible Edible scheme?

Jess said that she thought the scheme had been inspired by the guerrilla gardeners of Cuba, and while she knew that food crops had been planted in waste ground, on roundabouts and in flower beds and tubs throughout the town, she was unsure what the rules might be for harvesting the crops. Did the planters get first pick, or could anyone help themselves? The man explained that in fact a significant proportion of the previous year's crop had not been harvested, since many people were reticent about picking it.

"Well, that's a shame," said Jess, "Maybe you should publicise it better."

"Sure, we intend to this year," replied the man. "It's Nature's gift to the community, but if the community doesn't accept that gift, then Nature will take it away. Plants spoil, they get past their peak, they go to seed, onions bolt and so forth, so it's important that people realise that the food is available for all to take as required." Jess noted his American accent.

"Maybe you could provide recipes showing how to use the food, "said Jess, "After all not everyone knows how to cook an artichoke..."

"Well, would you know?" asked the man, in a challenging manner.

"No, I don't think I've ever been called upon to cook one," mused Jess, "but if I wanted to, I'd ask my son. He grew some once on his allotment."

"Your son has an allotment? Where is that?"

"In Bristol; I suppose the growing season is a bit longer there than here,"

"Well, in actual fact the growing season is lengthening, even here in the Pennines. It's all because of global warming. You'll have heard of the Gulf Stream? It's actually slowing down, so the warm water it brings is staying close to our shores for longer, and it's having a marked effect."

"We're rather a long way from the sea here, though," said Jess, doubtfully, wondering just exactly how the Gulf Stream effect might manage to penetrate Todmorden's steep narrow valleys.

"Yet even here the effects can still be noticed. After all, palm trees grow on the west side of the UK right up as far as the north of Scotland. I'm actually a scientist, and I came here years ago from LA to study climate change."

Jess was astonished to hear that someone had left California to move to landlocked Todmorden - and had apparently voluntarily remained.

"Oh, I love it here," said the man, as though reading her thoughts. "Sure, the valleys may get a little dark and claustrophobic in winter at times but the people here are great, and I have a family here now. Tell me, I hope you don't mind me saying, you're a person of middle years, as I am myself; do you recall when the food we ate was real, not pre-packed or processed or loaded with preservatives?"

"Yes, of course," said Jess, "But people had more time to prepare fresh food then, and not so many women went out to work. You can hardly blame people for wanting to make life a bit easier."

"But were you taught to cook, by your mother perhaps?"

"I was taught at school; I taught my mother to make jam."

"You see, people are leaving school these days without knowing how to cook. They don't know what to do with a carrot, let alone an artichoke. A generation has become de-skilled, lost confidence, and many of the cookery programmes on TV are served up as entertainment rather than being practical. There's more emphasis on who's going to survive to the next round, the dramas and tantrums, rather than the preparation of the food."

"Thank heavens for Delia, then" murmured Jess.

"Yes, she's great - but often those celebrity chefs claim their dishes are so simple, and then the list of ingredients turns out to be almost as long as the electoral roll. Those fellows are often filmed in exotic places cooking with exotic ingredients that ordinary not very confident cooks can't always relate to. Now, if they used local seasonal ingredients, people would have a better idea. Unfortunately, we're mostly in thrall to supermarkets these days..."

"My younger son gets a lot of food out of skips," said Jess. "And of course the elder one grows some of his own. They were both brought up near Hebden Bridge," she added by way of explanation.

The man nodded." Lots of alternative ways of living in this valley," he said, shaking Jess's hand as she prepared to leave.

Jess left the Town Hall just as a heavy shower was beginning. She took refuge in a café feeling in need of a pot of tea and a scone, after all this earnest discussion on the philosophy of food. Just as she was pouring her second cup, she noticed a group of people dressed for hiking, some carrying scallop shells, emerge from the church opposite. They were led by the Bishop of Wakefield, who was not wearing hiking gear, but was garbed in his usual purple attire, and sheltering under an umbrella held by an assistant. A photographer took several group pictures, after which the Bishop blessed the hikers, who then all trooped up the road in the direction of the moors. The Bishop was escorted back into the church by his umbrella bearer, while the photographer came across to the café.

"What's going on over there then?" the waitress asked the photographer as she served him with his latte.

"Pilgrims," said the photographer. "They're planning to follow in the steps of St. Paulinus and walk to York in a week. Don't envy them, they'll be soaked through long before they get to their first night's stop."

"Where's that?" asked the waitress.

"Berringden Brow church. But they were going over the tops first, to look at an old stone Paulinus cross up on the moors."

"It seems to be clearing up a bit now," remarked the waitress. Jess took this as her cue to leave. She was planning to walk back along the canal, a route far less rigorous than the path over the tops. She wished the pilgrims well and hoped that they would not fall into too many sloughs up there on the moors. Jess reflected that pilgrimage was not intended to be easy, and was certainly not to be undertaken by the faint-hearted, but she hoped that the beneficial effect of the Gulf Stream would quickly make itself manifest, and that the sun would soon be shining on the pilgrim band.

Nick turned up at Jess's house just as she arrived back home after her walk, bearing a covered dish which he placed in the fridge. As it was Sunday, he was expecting some food to be ready, but Jess had not had a chance to prepare anything, so she suggested they should go to the local pub, which served home-cooked food until eight o'clock. As they arrived, they found the dining area unusually full of people in hiking attire, some with scallop shells. The pilgrims had arrived in the village, and were seeking sustenance.

"How did you all get on? I saw you setting off in that heavy downpour," said Jess to the man sitting at the next table.

"Not very well; one lady had to be fetched home because it was too much for her, and then a man got into difficulties as we were up on the moors looking at the Paulinus cross, and we had to get the Search and Rescue people out to assist. He's been taken to hospital. He's in his eighties, and these steep moorland paths are bit of a shock, it's not like a walk in the park. So by the time we had waited for this chap to be rescued it was getting late, and we had to come on here by bus."
"Oh dear," said Jess. "Not quite what you'd planned, but what a good thing the buses were still running, although of course the public transport option wasn't open to St. Paulinus..."

"Never mind, we've nearly all of us got our bus passes," said the man cheerfully, as his plate of roast beef and Yorkshire puddings arrived. Jess reflected that she had probably walked further than the pilgrims had that day. She and Nick ate their roast dinners, but Nick told her not to order pudding, as there was a large apple crumble in the fridge back at her house. Since the closure of the advice centre, Nick was living an alternative life, as befits many a resident of the Berringden Valley. The large dish of apple crumble had been received in payment for work he had done for a grateful woman, whose Incapacity Benefit he had successfully argued should be restored. The appeal tribunal had agreed that her illness prevented her from working and the woman was so delighted that she had not only baked him the crumble but had also treated him to a poetry recitation in her kitchen.

"What were the poems about? And were they any good?"

"They were mostly about the difficulties she is having with her husband," said Nick. "They were quite good, but they did not rhyme or scan. They were free verse, I suppose."

"Like your services are free," said Jess. Nick did not need to earn, his mother had left a goodly sum and a paid-for house. His reluctance to renew the television licence brought him over to Jess's house where there was usually food available and he could watch "Match of the Day". He was now a free agent.

Chapter 34

My name is Charles, and I'm in here with Ada, my wife. We've been married since 1947. I was born in 1919 and Ada was born in 1920. She was in the next room to mine until recently, but she had to be moved downstairs because she has Alzheimer's and it's getting worse, and she was becoming harder to manage. It's really difficult for me to see her deteriorating, day by day. I go down to sit with her every morning, but she doesn't always realise who I am, even after all these years of marriage.

I was in the North African Desert during the war, and Ada was a land girl. We reached an understanding before I went away. I was taken prisoner, but Ada waited for me, despite getting other offers. I can't talk about my time in the war, I've spent years trying to put it all to the back of my mind. We finally got married in that dreadful winter of 1947, the worst on record. We had to fetch all the food for the reception on sledges, not that you could get much of anything. I had all sorts of jobs, but eventually we ended up managing a homeless shelter run by the church. We had all types of people –drug addicts, alcoholics, vagrants, mentally ill people, pregnant girls who'd been thrown out by their parents – Ada looked after that side of things of course, and the women were in a separate building. A church society took the babies away to be adopted, and sometimes the girls went back home to their families. Others stayed with us until they could find a job and sort their lives out.

Ada and I had four children, two boys and two girls, we were a happy family. We went away every summer to church camps in the countryside, the kids always had a great time. Now we've ten grand-kids, but Ada doesn't recognise any of them, and it's upsetting for them to visit. She's just not the person I lived with all those years, the illness changes your personality. She was always the kindest, sweetest, gentlest woman you could ever wish to meet, now she's so very different. You know, I'm finding this very difficult, I hope you won't mind if we finish now. Maybe I'll try to tell you a bit more another time.

The next time Jess was visiting the care home, Charles came to find her, and said he wanted to add to his life story account.

There's something I want to say, that you might find it interesting. We were way ahead of the times when it came to ideas about the environment. We always went to a spring to get water for the children to drink, because we never trusted what the authorities told us about chemicals in the public water supply. This was long before you could get all this bottled water. Now lots of people are raising questions about drinking water, with good reason, too, as fluoride is a rat poison. Imagine, they put fluoride, a rat poison in the public water supply; it's supposed to make the citizens more compliant. To think we fought Hitler and the Japs, only to have the water poisoned by our own government! People called us eccentric thirty years ago, but they don't say that so much now. I've always insisted that the kids and now the grand-kids should use non-fluoride toothpaste, I use it myself. They haven't had any more fillings than those who use the other stuff.

I discovered that I have a gift for healing, it was quite by accident, and I've never exploited it. I don't advertise, people come to me by word of mouth. If only I could heal Ada! I suppose it works partly because people believe it will, but of course, Ada can't do that. I can't heal a sceptic or someone who cannot understand', people have to know what is happening and have faith. I lay my hands on the people who come to me, and a certain power is channelled through me. I don't know why I was chosen to have this ability, and feel very humble that I have been able to help so many poorly people.

Ada was always a great one for home remedies, she used comfrey, and drank cider vinegar and honey. Everyone knows dock leaves to take the pain out of nettle stings – well – she knew lots more country lore, from her time as a land girl, when the farmer's wife taught her how to make country wines and jams and jellies and pickles and potions and such. And all that's coming back into fashion again now, I believe, what with the recession, and those TV programmes about wild foods. It's such a pity that Ada can't appreciate it; the real Ada's gone for good .,, Such a shame you never got the chance to know her.

Chapter 35

Jess's neighbour, Mark, was fixing the kitchen light for her. Jess always struggled with any household maintenance task which involved climbing step-ladders, since she became dizzy once past the second rung. Over the years, Jess had employed many different handymen, but they always seemed to disappear after a while. One had got a job so was no longer available, while another had become incapacitated after falling off his motorbike. A third had suffered a nervous breakdown, while another moved away from the area after his marriage was dissolved. Jess had eventually found a really pleasant man, who had advertised his services in the local paper. He came once to fix up a curtain pole, and Jess had wanted him to return the following week to decorate the attic. However, he failed to arrive as agreed, so Jess had telephoned him. It took her several attempts before he answered, and when she did eventually get through, the man was talking in whispers.

"I can't come to you again, my girlfriend objects to me going to any houses where there are single women," said the man, sotto voce.

"But didn't you explain to her that we would be chaperoned at all times by a Staffordshire Bull terrier?" asked Jess.

"I can't talk now, she's just coming in from the garden..." and the phone went dead. Jess sighed, yet another handyman was failing to live up to his name. And wasn't it illegal to discriminate in the provision of goods or services on the grounds of marital status? Jess thought it probably was. The last time she had been refused a service on the grounds that she was single had been years ago when the hospital consultant refused to sterilize her.

"But your domestic situation is so unsettled," Dr. McGregor had said'

No, it isn't," said Jess. "I am very happily settled with my two young sons. It's just that I don't ever, under any circumstances, want to find myself unexpectedly pregnant again. I'm thirty-five and trying to be responsible.". Dr. McGregor sighed. "One day, you will meet a man, and he will want you to marry him and give him children...."

"And I'll have two perfectly lovely ones to give him!"

"No, no; he will want you to give him children of his own! If you were married, then that would be different, I would perform the laparoscopy."

By now, Jess was becoming rather annoyed. She had come for a medical consultation, not to have her fortune told. Just where was this mythical man, anyway? She felt like asking if he would be tall dark and handsome... Jess wanted to point out that just because a woman was currently married, it did not necessarily mean that she would not later possibly be divorced. Lots of people were these days, so who could be said to be truly settled? Then another thought struck her.

"I can assure you that I would have nothing whatsoever to do with any man who did not love and accept my sons."
"But men want their own children, not those of others! This is the case throughout Nature. For example, lions who become the dominant male in the pride kill any cubs fathered by the previous dominant male when they take over the lionesses. No, only married women should be sterilized."

89

First astrology, now natural history, but no proper discussion of gynaecology, which was Jess had actually come for. She got up to leave. She later reported back to her own GP, who seemed to find the whole thing rather amusing.

"Whatever century is old McGregor living in? Don't worry, I'll send you somewhere else. I'm sure Mr. Jones will be more obliging."

Mr. Jones had indeed agreed that a laparoscopy was a sensible solution in Jess's circumstances. Jess felt that provision of health services was not so much a post-code lottery as a matter of finding a doctor with a post – enlightenment frame of mind.
So now Mark was fixing the kitchen light, which needed a new starter, and Jess would repay him with a jar of her home-made blackcurrant jam. Jess had explained about the handyman with the possessive girlfriend, and Mark had laughed and said that he doubted whether such a wimpish character would still be in business. He was probably now living as a kept man - after all, it was likely to be single women who were most in need of the services of a handyman, since the married ones would no doubt prevail upon their husbands to do any required repairs.

"Of course, some women are more than capable of doing DIY, and there are lots of specialist Women's DIY services in Hebden Bridge, women plumbers, decorators, electricians. I just wish I didn't feel giddy every time I climbed a ladder..."

"Never mind, your jam is always delicious, and we can't all be good at everything," said Mark, switching on the light.

Jess was taking Mash for a teatime stroll when she spotted Dolly back in her enclosure. Dolly noticed them, but instead of running over to the fence and greeting them, Dolly simply gave a quick "Baa!" and carried on munching grass. She had only been way for a few weeks, but during that time she seemed to have grown from a lamb into a sheep. Her owners appeared, and said that Dolly had enjoyed her stay with their friends, who had even allowed her into the house to watch TV.
 "No wonder she's seems disgruntled, back in a chilly field."

In other local livestock news, the progress of Paul and Naomi's peacocks was disappointing; the peahen was still valiantly sitting, but none of the eggs had hatched, so it appeared that they had been infertile all along. It seemed that the peacock was all bluster and style rather than substance and delivery, like so many of the men Jess had known over the years. Naomi took the eggs away while the peahen was absent from the nest having her food, and a surprised honking ensued when the bird returned. The peacock wandered over to see what the noise was about, then escorted his mate back to the greenhouse. Jess felt sorry for the would-be mother, and hoped that she would have better luck next year.

Chapter 36

I'll tell you something about my life. My wife's out just now. You'll have gathered that this particular care home has many retired clergymen – priests, missionaries, that sort of person. Not that this means that we all live together in perfect peace and harmony; we may all be Christian, but we're from all the different denominations, and we are a very mixed bag of people. I'm Dennis, and I'm a retired Catholic priest; you look surprised, quite understandably, because I mentioned my wife. Well, some members of the Church of England did not care for the ordination of women, and came over to Rome. I was one of that number and because I was married, my wife came with me. You may have heard on the radio and television the on-going debate about the celibacy of Catholic priests. I find that as a family man, people can relate to me in a different way to an unmarried priest. But others prefer their clergymen to be celibate, and that's fine. People can choose. In my case, the ordination of women was simply the tip of the iceberg; I had been moving away from certain aspects of Church of England for some time before female ordination was mooted. I was the vicar of St. Luke's and various changes were suggested to ensure we were more 'accessible' to both our communicants and the wider parish. One idea was that in the service of Holy Communion, we should no longer receive the host at the altar, but place a table in the aisle and stand around it to receive. My congregation preferred kneeling at the altar, that was what they wanted or were used to. Then we were advised to 'up-date' our selection of hymns, we were told to use more 'Happy-clappy' tunes, preferably accompanied by guitars. St. Luke's had always had a fine tradition of sacred and choral music, which people were used to; indeed, many were attracted to our services because of the wonderful music. We did get a few more families coming to Morning Prayer as a result of the changes, but the older folk began staying away. They did not care for screaming babies or boisterous toddlers rushing around the church during the service. And of course, we had a very good primary school, which everyone locally wanted their children to attend, so I fear some parents came solely for spurious reasons. Don't get me wrong; the church should welcome everyone, young and old, 'ancient and modern' so to speak. We are a broad church, and should be able to provide a variety of services to accommodate all preferences with regard to worship. I really dislike the 'one size fits all' approach. However, these new people began demanding that their children be baptised, in order that they could be considered for a place at the primary school. I am always delighted to welcome a child into God's family, but, in my view, at least one of those chosen to stand as a godparent to a candidate for baptism must have been confirmed, and it was hard for many parents to find anyone suitable. And the get-ups some of those godmothers wore! Backless, strapless –I almost said topless - dresses, more suited to an evening out clubbing, or Ladies Day at the races, than to a religious sacrament. Then people seemed to think it was their right to remarry in church after a divorce, or even after several divorces, and I'm afraid I have always been firmly against that. It was my right to decide who could be married in my own church. I always offered the couple the option of a church blessing on their union, after the civil ceremony, but that was not good enough for some. St. Luke's was in an attractive location, and many people seemed to be more concerned about the wedding photos and videos than the actual service. Fortunately, it was about then that all these new wedding venues opened up, in stately homes and country house hotels, which took the pressure off St. Luke's, and we went back to holding weddings for those who truly wanted a religious ceremony.

However, the next people to target the church were people wanting bogus marriages, usually male asylum seekers, whose cases had failed on appeal, wanting to marry young Eastern European women. They frequently had no common language, and clearly did not understand anything of the sacred nature of what they were promising. The 'best man' was usually a gang-master/fixer type, who would think nothing of using his mobile phone during the ceremony, and the bride's attire was often something like jeans and a duffel coat. The couple would go their separate ways immediately they left the church porch. After one or two of these farcical marriages, I

*realised what was happening and began turning them away, because it
seemed quite wrong to me. The service would have had no meaning, it
would simply be a way of circumventing the immigration laws The Mr. Fix-
its got rather shirty with me, but I told them that everyone I married should
at least know and be able to pronounce the name of their spouse. I began to
resent having to act as an arm of the immigration service and notified the
appropriate authorities. I had to, in order to protect myself, as some poor
vicars were being arrested for conducting these marriages, at least one was
sent to jail! The local Mr. Fix-it was arrested and sent for trial, it was all
written up in the Berringden Bugle recently, you might have seen it. Then
someone pointed out to me that the writer CS Lewis – you know, he wrote
the Narnia chronicles - had agreed to marry the American poet Ruth
Gresham in order that she could remain in this country. They had a civil
ceremony but fell in love later; the story is told in the film, "Shadowlands"
with Anthony Hopkins and Debra Winger. She became terminally ill, and
they subsequently had a religious service at her hospital bedside. So, as
they say, there is nothing new under the sun, although it seems to be on a
completely different scale these days.*

*I'm afraid I finally had to leave the Church of England over the issue of
gay clergy. We had one such priest in a neighbouring parish, living with his
friend in the Vicarage, and, I had to attend deanery meetings with this man.
On a personal level, he was a charming chap; but I had so many relevant
passages of Scripture running through my head every time I saw him, it was
all I could do to stop myself quoting them at him. Sodom and Gomorrah
etc. I asked the Rural Dean to say something, but he was a laid-back sort of
person, who said that he could find no fault at all with this gay priest's
ministry, so it was left at that. Naturally, my wife was rather anxious about
coming over to Catholicism, as she had played an important role as Vicar's
wife in our C. of E days, and was unsure what there might be for her to do
in the Roman Catholic church. But there are always flowers to be
arranged, jumble sales to prepare for, cakes to be baked and so forth. She's
an accomplished musician, and so was able to suggest suitable music for
the services, and run the youth orchestra. She managed to carve out a role
for herself eventually. But as she would certainly tell you, if she were here,
in all honesty, it really isn't the same...*

Chapter 37

Jess was heading back to the West Country to steward at the Combe Salterton Folk Festival. She had originally volunteered to work on the gate of the Craft Fair field in the afternoons, but only last week the organisers had rung to ask if she would be prepared to act as chaperone for a Korean dance troupe. This would be full-time, and would necessitate staying in a university hostel with the team rather than camping. The original chaperone had backed out, and it was important that each visiting dance team had someone with then at all times, to guide them around the various venues, escort them to where meals were to be served, ensure they boarded the correct bus, and generally assist with any difficulties which might arise.

"But I don't speak Korean!" exclaimed Jess. The organisers explained that she would not need to, since the team was bringing its own interpreter. Jess had a good knowledge of Combe Salterton, since she had attended the folk festival on many previous occasions, including as child with her mother, when they had gone down to the coast for day trips since Dotey had not been a camping sort of person. In those days, the festival had been a much smaller event, but Jess could recall hearing the exotic sound of Andean Pan pipes for the first time, (before they could be heard playing in seemingly every shopping centre in the land), and joining in the country dancing with the Chingford Boys Morris.

The Koreans' flight had been delayed, and there were severe hold-ups on the motorway, so they did not arrive until almost midnight. Unfortunately, there was no sign of the promised interpreter, so the room allocation was rather a muddle. There were 45 Koreans in the dance troupe, far more than Jess had been expecting. Jess then received a text message saying that the interpreter would not be arriving until the next day. Eventually, everyone found somewhere to sleep. By this time, it was gone one o'clock, and Jess was exhausted. She was already regretting having agreed to be a chaperone.

Jess shepherded her team to the refectory for breakfast the next morning. Everyone was looking rather glum, and the dancers appeared not to care very much for the food. After breakfast, they went to meet the bus, and immediately, faces fell at the sight of the ordinary double-decker bus chartered by the frugal festival organisers instead of the luxury coach the Koreans clearly felt they deserved. There was considerable difficulty getting all the team's equipment, which included several enormous drums and gongs and an assortment of unusual stringed instruments, not to mention 46 people, onto the bus. In the middle of all the loading and stowing and repacking a young woman arrived; she turned out to be the interpreter, and the daughter of the troupe leader, Madame C. She was clearly horrified at the transport arrangements, and after listening to a tirade in Korean from her mother, she explained to Jess in imperious tones that Madame C wished Jess to be aware that neither the food nor the transport was at all to her liking or expectations, and would Jess please do something about it quickly. Jess replied that she was just a chaperone, and had no power to change anything; all she could do would be to relay Madame's complaints to the organisers.

Just what sort of a holiday job was this turning out to be, thought Jess, her tact and patience already stretched to the limit. To make matters worse, the day was becoming unbearably hot, and the bus did not of course possess air conditioning. Most of the other overseas teams appeared to be meekly falling in with their chaperones' directions, except for the Ghanaian drummers who were evidently running on African time, and were yet to put in an appearance. Tim, their chaperone, and his bus driver were sighing with exasperation, and Jess was somewhat comforted by the fact that she was not the only one having problems with her team.

Eventually, all the drums, gongs, fans, dresses, dragon costumes, musical instruments and other paraphernalia had been loaded onto the baking bus, and they all set off on the short journey down to the coast. The morning's rehearsal and sound checks appeared to go quite well, but Jess's heart sank when she saw the left-over lunches. Everyone had to eat at the rugby club, but it was apparent that pie and chips did not appeal to the Korean palate, especially during a heat-wave. Some of the dancers were so slim, Jess wondered if they ate anything at all, and feared that they might disappear altogether after a week of the rugby club diet. She politely asked the club catering manager if salad could be provided in future. He looked at her as if she were mad, and replied that he did not get much call for salad, being used to providing substantial fare for burly rugby players, but that he would try to get some the following day; however, these Korean folkies must understand that it was a set meal, and they must either like it or lump it. Jess dreaded having to explain all this to Madame C and Miss Interpreter, who kept going off into voluble huddles, emerging only to glare at Jess.

By the third day, complete strangers were coming up to Jess and telling her how tired she looked. Jess was indeed absolutely shattered, as a result of the Koreans' almost ceaseless demands. Absolutely nothing about the festival was right for them, it appeared, and they did not seem inclined to make the best of a bad situation. Then Jess was constantly anxious that she might lose a team member as she led them through the crowded streets from the various performances to meal venues and back to the bus stop. The young dancers had a habit of becoming distracted and wandering off in the wrong direction, which meant that Jess frequently had to halt the main party and go in search of stragglers. To cap it all, there had been an unwelcome development the previous night, when a chambermaid at the student hostel had accosted Jess, sobbing her heart out, and explaining that her digital camera had disappeared. She thought she must have left it in one of the rooms she had been cleaning.

"I'm sorry, it's not my problem, better tell the manager, Mike isn't it?"

"I did that, but he said I should speak to you. I think the camera is in one of your dancers' rooms, but I'm not sure which one...."

"Well, I'll ask the interpreter to have a word with the team, and if anyone finds it, I'll let you know." Jess wrote down the chambermaid's number, feeling cross, since it was not really anything to do with her, and she had enough to worry about already. Silly girl, fancy taking a camera to work... Another distraction was the burgeoning romance between one of the Korean musicians and a member of the backstage crew at the main performance arena. The lack of any common language did not seem to affect their billing and cooing, and Jess became concerned that the young woman might decided to defect in order to stay with her Devonian lover, that Jess might somehow be held responsible for an international incident. That afternoon, there was a procession of all the international dance teams along the sea front ,and since the weather was still scorching, the poor dragon dancers were on the verge of heat exhaustion. Jess made sure that she was on hand with bottles of mineral water for the two young men as they emerged from the heavy costume. They were grateful and Madame nodded approvingly, but Miss Interpreter continued to look down her nose.

That night, Jess was too hot to sleep, finally nodding off well after midnight. At one o'clock, she was woken by the sound of frantic knocking at her door. Thinking that some calamity must have befallen one of the Koreans, Jess grabbed her dressing gown and rushed to open the door to find the chambermaid.

"I wonder if you found my camera...."

Jess almost slammed the door in her face in fury.

"Go away! I told you I would ring you if it turned up!"

"So you haven't found it, then...."

"No! Goodnight!" Jess closed the door and tried to get back to sleep, but couldn't, what with the heat and her bad temper.
The following morning Jess went in search of hostel manager Mike. He was nowhere to be found. Jess, possibly by this time the most exhausted and furious guest ever to stay at the university, told his staff members that they must phone him and get him to come from wherever he was at once, and miraculously, Mike appeared within five minutes. Jess fulminated about being a paying guest, and her right to quiet enjoyment of her room, which meant not being disturbed by the chambermaid on a fool's errand in the small hours. She reminded Mike that the folk festival contract was worth a lot of money, and that guests should be treated with consideration. The missing camera had not turned up, but that was not her responsibility. Mike agreed that the chambermaid had been out of order, and offered Jess extra teabags and sachets of milk, by way of recompense for her disturbed night. Jess flounced out of Mike's office to attend to her team, but the day which had got off to such a bad start was about to get even worse.

When the bus appeared round the corner and drew up outside the hostel, the Ghanaian drummers were already aboard. Generally, each team had its own bus, but the driver explained that today there was a shortage of buses, so teams would have to double up. Miss Interpreter recoiled in horror when Jess explained the situation to her, and refused point blank either to board the bus, or to allow any of her team members to do so. She demanded that Jess procure another bus.

"Come on, we can all get on this one if we squash up, it's not so bad now that the instruments are down at Combe already," said Jess. But the Koreans would not budge, and Madame was issuing a torrent of furious instructions to her daughter, who was regarding the Africans with distaste. "Jess you get us another bus! We cannot be expected to share with them!"

Meanwhile, the Ghanaians were expressing their views equally forcefully.

"Jess, you must make them get on this bus with us! Their attitude hurts us very much, and the way they look at us. We are not animals!"

Jess boarded the bus and sat down next to Daniel the Ghanaian team leader. She wondered where Tim, the drummers' chaperone was, but Daniel explained that he had already left for Combe Salterton by car. Jess waited. The bemused driver wanted to know whether he should set off, but Jess asked him not to go yet. The Koreans sat down on the grass and there appeared to be a complete stand-off. Daniel, meanwhile, was pouring out his fury.

"Jess, I have worked with Paul McCartney, and with Eric Clapton, I have worked all over the world, but never have I been so insulted!"

His partner, Maria, tugged at Jess's sleeve and chimed in. "Yes, it hurts, us deeply, it hurts us here in our hearts!" Jess noticed there were tears in her eyes. She took Maria's hand.

"I know; what they are doing is absolutely inexcusable. It's not the young dancers so much as the leaders, Madame and her snooty daughter..."

Jess gazed levelly at the interpreter, and reminded her that she would be in breach of contract if she failed to get her team onto the bus. The haughty young woman finally backed down and shepherded the Koreans aboard, Jess noticed that they were all taking care to avoid sitting next to any of the Africans, some of whom had spare seats next to them. Jess signalled to the driver that he could at last depart.

Of course, they were very late arriving at Combe Salterton, and two of the festival officials were anxiously looking out for them. One officious man began telling Jess off as she leapt from the bus, but Jess forestalled him by announcing her resignation from her post as voluntary team chaperone, with immediate effect, unless someone could be sent to assist her forthwith.

"Oh, but there's no-one free, you'll just have to manage as best you can."

"Fine then, I quit, it's a thankless task, and it's meant to be my holiday!"

The organisers looked at one another. "No, wait; you just get them to the 'Meet the Teams' venue and we'll try to send someone over."

Jess was not altogether surprised when a disgruntled young –ish looking man appeared at the' Meet the Teams' tent, and announced that his name was Richard, and that he had been called away from his very important work in the publicity office simply because she could not mange her team! When Jess recounted the events of the morning, and indicated the throng of Korean musicians and dancers, Richard appeared to relent somewhat.

"Hmm, that sort of behaviour's not really in the spirit of the festival – and there does seem to be an awful lot of them..."

"Forty-six! And the interpreter thinks she's royalty and I'm something the cat's brought in! I keep telling her that I'm only a volunteer, but she seems to think I'm the one responsible for not getting them a luxury coach."

"Maybe you've made a mistake there, because it's possible that volunteers are treated in a lowly way in Korea, perhaps a bit like a serf or skivvy..."

However, it took only one glance at Richard and the interpreter became putty in his hands. Jess supposed he was quite attractive, in a long-haired, middle-ageing hippy-ish kind of way, and the interpreter clearly thought he was the bees' knees. Jess was so glad she had stuck up for herself.

Chapter 38

With Richard leading the troupe and Jess bringing up the rear, Jess was far less anxious about losing anyone, since she was quickly able to round up any stragglers. The rugby club catering manager had at last managed to procure some salad, and altogether the second half of the week seemed set to pass much more pleasantly than the first, much to Jess's relief.

The Koreans were not required to perform on the Wednesday, they would be at leisure, and Miss Interpreter had told Jess that they were planning to go shopping in Exeter. Jess was looking forward to a much needed day off, when Tim, the Ghanaian team chaperone, approached her at the hostel, and asked if she could look after the drummers the following day, as he had been called away to attend the funeral of a close relative. Since Jess's was the only international team not required, she would be the only chaperone with free time, so she felt she had no option but to agree. The Ghanaians would be unlikely to give her any trouble, and the only problem Jess could foresee would be ensuring the laid-back Africans were on time for the bus.

"What are we going to do tomorrow?" asked Richard. "We've both got the day off, so let's make to most of it. Let's go somewhere – anywhere except Combe Salterton, that is."

Jess explained that she would be chaperoning the Ghanaians.

"You've given up your day off? Jess, you're a saint! Looks like I'd better pitch in to help you with the drummers then."

"There's really no need, there are not that many of them and they all speak English. And I thought you would want to go back to the publicity office."

"No fear, I was glad to escape! Much more fun being out and about with you and our forty-six Far Eastern friends! "

(Hmm, he's changed his tune since Monday, thought Jess).

"Well, I'll see you first thing tomorrow, we could have a bit of a job getting them up bright and early for the bus, so you might be glad of me to go and drag Daniel and his pals out of bed. Sleep well, Jess!"

As Richard had predicted, Jess was indeed glad of his help with organising the Ghanaians, but once they were all safely on the bus, Jess felt that she could relax. They were just so much nicer to work with than her team, and for the first time that week, Jess began to enjoy herself. The drumming display, accompanied by a traditional dance by Maria and two other young women, was wonderful, and the audience at the 'Meet the Teams' tent applauded loudly. In the afternoon there was a workshop on the lawn outside the Pavilion, where Daniel and his team were teaching children how to drum. There was very little for Jess to do except sit in the sun and relax. She must have nodded off for a short while, but woke up to find Richard smiling down at her.

"Come on Jess, let's go for a walk along the prom. Everyone's fine here, they won't need us until tea time."

"But we shouldn't really leave them..."

"Of course we can, look I'll tell Maria we'll be way for half an hour. And if disaster should strike, they can always get you on your mobile phone."

Jess and Richard made their way down to the promenade. It was the first chance Jess had had all week to look at the various stalls selling clothes, hats, tie-dye scarves, souvenirs, sweets, paper flowers, musical instruments, and assorted seaside novelties. There were also fortune tellers, tattoo artists, face painters and performances of all kinds, including the West Dorset accordion players, Morris dancers, clog dancers, long-sword dancers, rapper-sword dancers, uni-cyclists, sword- swallowers and fire jugglers. Jess was marvelling at how the fire jugglers coped with so many flaming firebrands when she realised that Richard was not with her; however, he reappeared almost at once with two ice-creams and handed her one.
"It's got a dollop of clotted cream on top, thought you could do with a little luxury after all the running around you've had to do so far this week."

"Thank you," smiled Jess, thinking how nice it was for someone not to suppose she might be dieting or in need of a low fat option. She was relieved to find that Devonshire clotted cream was still being made and had not been outlawed by some government or European health directive.

This has been the best day of the festival so far, thought Jess; it can actually be fun being a chaperone, if you have a pleasant bunch of people to deal with, not a couple of prima donnas with their enormous entourage.

The remainder of the festival rushed by, and soon it was time for the final night's grand concert. After the Koreans had performed, an English folk ensemble took to the stage. The compère announced that their manager had first appeared at Combe Salterton in the 1960s with the Chingford Boys Morris, but Jess did not recognise him...

Jess anxiously counted Korean heads as the torch-light procession would its way down the hill from the arena to the seafront, where there was to be a huge firework finale. The young woman musician was reluctantly tearing herself way from her back-stage beau; and Madame was smiling serenely, no doubt pleased at the prospect of leaving Combe Salterton the following day, while Miss Interpreter was trying to flirt with Richard, whom Jess suspected might possibly be gay, since he seemed to be showing more interest in the male dragon dancers than Miss Snooty.

At last, the final torch was doused in the sea, the second maroon signalled the end of the fireworks and the last gasps of admiration faded on the sea breeze. The seagulls emerged from wherever they had been hiding during the spectacle, and recommenced their wheeling and squawking. It was time for Jess and Richard to round up their team and get them onto the bus one last time. Back at the hostel, Madame presented Jess with a pretty Korean fan, bearing her autograph, but Jess was more touched when Ghanaian Daniel came to find her and quietly gave her a lovely African bead bracelet in recognition of her support for his team during the shared bus stand-off.

Since the Koreans' flight was early the next morning, they were leaving at once for Heathrow, travelling overnight on a luxury coach rather than a despised service bus. Jess watched them load their drums, gongs, costumes, fans and instruments onto the coach, which was crammed full, with Madame taking the last seat. Jess and Richard waved them down the drive.

"What shall we do tomorrow, Jess?"

"Oh, I shall just have a quiet day recovering after all the excitement, then my friend and her little daughter are arriving on the teatime train, and we're having a few days by the sea. I suppose you are off back to Manchester?"

 "Not until the evening. Sounds like we'll both be at a loose end during the day. We could take a boat trip! We'll be back before your friends arrive."

Jess had been looking forward to a day doing very little after her hectic week, but she liked boat trips, and she thought it might seem churlish not to keep Richard company after he had been such a help for the past few days. Early next morning, they went down to the harbour, and found that there was an excursion about to leave, sailing along the Jurassic coast to Lyme Regis. Richard insisted on paying for Jess; she protested, but eventually they reached a compromise with Jess telling him that she would buy lunch.

The weather was still hot, but at sea there were cooling breezes, and the leisurely boat trip gave passengers an opportunity to view the magnificent coastal scenery, including red cliffs, secluded bays, and sea stacks. At one point, the commentator announced that they would shortly be passing a naturist beach, and there was a rush by passengers to find their binoculars. However, Jess was more interested in the sea-bird colonies along the coast.

Jess had always loved Lyme Regis. She had been there first as a child, and later with her own sons, who had enjoyed looking for fossils and going mackerel fishing. Over a delicious lunch in one of the cafés, Richard told Jess about his job in Manchester, teaching at a school for pupils, who for various reasons, had been excluded from mainstream education. Jess thought it sounded like very hard work. There was not much time for Jess to tell Richard about her life, because they had to be sure not to miss the boat back. The cashier gave Jess a sidelong glance when she went to pay the bill.

"I hope you and your son enjoyed your meal..."

"My son?" Jess was quite startled, wondering where Tom had sprung from.

"The young man you're with – oh, so he's not your son? Of course, if he was, you'd have been a teenage mum, I don't mean that you look **that** old."

"We're simply colleagues," laughed Jess, wondering why it was necessary to have to explain this to a silly restaurant cashier. She returned to the table, where Richard was picking up his rucksack.

"Thanks, Jess, that was a great lunch. Well, we'd better get back down to the harbour, don't want to miss the boat. Anyway, what's so amusing?"

"That woman at the cash desk thought you were my son for some reason."

"She must need her eyes tested! Anyone can see you're not old enough."

"She did say I must have been a gymslip mother. But it's really no business of hers who's dining with who. Just out of interest, how old are you?"

"I'm forty." Jess was surprised to hear that Richard was as old as that.

"Well, as it happens, she was quite right, I would have been a teenage mum - but I'm not saying how far into my teens I was when you were born..."

"Oh, really, I would never have thought it, to me you look younger every time I see you, now you haven't got forty-six Koreans to worry about!"

With that, Richard put his arm affectionately around Jess and swept her out of the restaurant, winking broadly at the cashier as they passed her desk.

Jess felt sleepy on the return trip; she settled down for a short nap, and was surprised when she woke to find herself leaning against Richard's shoulder.

"Wake up Jess, we're almost back in port!"

"No, are we really? I must have been asleep much longer than I thought!"

"A good three-quarters of an hour - not surprising, after such a busy week."

"Well, it was quite hard work. I would never have managed to last out to the end without your help, Richard, thanks so much. You saved my sanity."

"I've enjoyed it enormously, you rescued me from a stuffy office and I rescued you from the white slave trade....seriously, you drew the short straw with that particular team, maybe the previous chaperone backed out because she had an idea how difficult they could be. But at least you've had today to relax, before your friends arrive from Leeds."

"It's been a lovely day, thanks so much for suggesting it. Now, I had better get over to the station, to meet Sehlile and Mia."
"I'll come with you. I'm on the tea-time train to Manchester."

As the Leeds train drew in, Richard pulled Jess close to him and kissed her.

"See you very soon, Jess, I'll ring you when we're both back up North, I promise. Take care of yourself and try to relax after your difficult week!"

Jess watched him cross the footbridge, then went to meet Sehlile and Mia, who were approaching along the platform. More hugs all round, and Mia presented Jess with a drawing of a cat which she had done on the long train journey. There had apparently been a cat on the train, travelling in a basket.

"Who was that attractive man I saw you with just now?" asked Sehlile.

"Oh, that was Richard, he's been helping me with the team chaperoning."

"It looked like the two of you needed a team of chaperones yourselves..."

"Ha-ha! Now, let's get to the youth hostel, I've booked us into a family room, and then we'll see about some tea!" Jess was very surprised at the affectionate manner of Richard's parting –maybe he wasn't gay after all.

It was Sehlile and Mia's first trip to the West Country, and Jess was kept busy over the next few days, showing them the delights of Devon, so she had very little time to think about Richard. They had exchanged mobile phone numbers in the course of their team chaperoning duties, but even so, Jess did not really expect to hear from him again. Over the years, several men had promised to phone, but hardly any of them ever did; and Jess had noted that it seemed to be always the odd ones that actually got around to phoning while those she would have been quite glad to hear from invariably remained silent. A promise to phone was simply a polite way to take one's leave, meaning nothing to most men although women set more store by it.

Chapter 39

Back in Yorkshire after the holidays, Jess was surprised to find a large pink orthopaedic chair in her sitting room. When Alex appeared she asked him if he knew anything about it, or the broken pane of glass in the kitchen door.

"Oh, Kate told me and me mate to fetch it here. She said you could make use of it, cos she and Adrian have ordered a new suite. But it weighs a ton, we had a right job manoeuvring it, and we accidentally broke the glass."

Kate appeared. "Hello Jess, welcome home; what do you think of your new chair? We simply had to get rid of it, so of course I thought of you....look, I'll show you how it works – you sit in it and pull this lever and hey presto, the footrest comes up and you can lie right back and relax." As Kate demonstrated, the chair suddenly expanded to take up almost half the room.

"Well, thank you, but I'm not sure it's really quite what I want..."

"Now, Jess you really mustn't look a gift horse in the mouth as my mother always says. It will simply go for scrap if you don't use it, and that would be such a waste, it's still in quite good condition. I shall have to ask the council to take it away."

"But there are charitable furniture schemes which collect unwanted goods and redistribute them to those who want stuff; doesn't the RSPCA do it? Why don't you check with them?"

"Really, Jess, I don't have time for that! You lucky, lucky single girls have so much more time for that sort of thing! Speaking of which, I'd better be getting back to Adrian, he'll be wondering what's become of me."

As Jess was preparing to resume work she found herself wondering what had happened to May over the summer, so she rang Anna to ask whether there had been any developments.

"No-one's able to see her," said Anna. "She's in a coma now, only her sons and the carers can go in. The end won't be long now, I'm afraid."

"Her sons? They're here now?"

"As soon as May lapsed into a coma the care-home manager called them. She was no longer in a position to object, and they are her flesh and blood."

"And have you met them? What do they think about May and John?"

"Yes, they asked to see me, and thanked me for befriending their mother. They said it must have been difficult, and they actually sent a generous donation to the befriending scheme, which was good of them."

"They obviously appreciated your hard work. Let's hope the scheme gives you someone easier next. But what about John? Is he still on the scene?"

"No, not now there's no prospect of any more money. Imogen tells me he's had another woman waiting quietly in the wings all along, and they've just been hanging around until May dies before moving in together."

"Didn't John manage to get a solicitor to come to the care home and alter May's Will? Won't he get everything that's left?"

"I think the sons are planning to contest it, they claim that she was not of sound mind when it was drawn up. The case could be quite lengthy – these things often are, and I don't imagine John will want to hang around wasting money fighting a protracted legal action. I think he'll leave soon, as all May's pensions and allowances will all dry up the minute she dies."

Jess reflected that she should leave clear instructions for Tom and Alex to the effect that if she should ever lose her mind and fall in love with a man of dubious intent half her age, they should have her immediately certified.

On the subject of younger men, it was now almost two weeks since Jess had returned from Devon, and there was no escaping the realisation that Richard had not kept his word about ringing her very soon. In many ways, Jess was not surprised, since she knew that men often make promises they subsequently fail to keep. It was just that she had hoped and believed that Richard might be different, that he would turn out to possess that commodity all too rare in most of the men she had known in her life - sincerity.

Jess then wondered if she should ring Richard. She was due to go to Manchester soon to attend the première of Evan's new play, about the web of relationships between a prostitute, her younger sister, a school-boy, his teacher and the teacher's wife. This was to be held in at a city centre hotel in a couple of weeks' time. Jess wondered whether Richard might be interested in going, and decided that it would not hurt to ring and ask him.

After all, things had moved on from the days a generation since, when her mother had instructed her never, on any account, to chase after a man.

"If he's interested, let him make the running," had been Dotey's mantra. "It's a man's job to do the chasing and it simply cheapens a girl to run after men, it destroys her reputation."

Jess thought this advice sounded so quaint nowadays, after all, men and women were meant to be equal, and a middle-aged mother-of-two such as herself could not really be said to have much of a reputation left to protect. And after all, nothing ventured, nothing gained. She had Richard's number stored in n her mobile phone address book, and rang it. Immediately, the voice-mail message cut in; obviously Richard was busy. Jess hesitated a little, then left what she hoped was a friendly message, telling him that she was coming over the Manchester soon, and asking if he would care to attend the world première of a new play; if so would he please contact her so she could reserve a ticket for him.

A few days later Anna rang Jess to say that May had passed away, and that the funeral was to be the following Tuesday afternoon. May's sons had asked Anna to go, since they did not think there would be many people there, and Anna wondered if Jess would come, to make up the numbers. May had never had many friends, and she had alienated most of the other care home residents with her strict views about not playing Bingo or doing the lottery, although a few of the care workers had agreed to go. Jess did not really want to attend, she had scarcely known May, having interviewed her on just the one occasion, and it seemed a bit like rent-a-crowd. However, she wanted to support Anna, so she agreed to go.

"Just to the church service then, not the funeral tea," said Jess, thinking that she could always give the excuse of having to get back to walk Mash.

The day was fine, and the simple service went well. May's elder son gave the eulogy, which concentrated on May's earlier life, and made no mention of her more recent escapade with John the conman. Jess had wondered if he would be there, but Anna said that he had been expressly forbidden to attend by May's sons, and Imogen had told her that he was preparing to move in with the woman who had been patiently waiting in the wings all this time. She lived on a remote moorland farm high above the Berringden Valley, and John was planning to start a new life with, as a sheep-farmer.

"May never got to wear those nighties," said Anna, as they made their way out of the church and towards the cemetery. "And I had such a job to find them. I finally tracked a couple down in that old draper's shop, they were having a closing-down sale. No-one else in the care home wants to wear winceyette, because it's always so warm in there, so I think I'll take them to the Pop-In shop. Someone will probably be glad of them when it's winter."

"Has the scheme allocated you a new person to befriend?" asked Jess.

"Well, they keep suggesting people, but I don't think I can face any more befriending at present. I'd like to have a break from it for a while. You don't feel appreciated, you can be put upon, and taken for granted if you're not careful. Then the client sacks you, next they want you back again, you may have to bite your tongue at their outlandish opinions...there's often a good reason why some people are lonely, they're just not that easy to get on with... I suppose I'm feeling rather jaded. I think I might try to get a proper job, like you, and give voluntary work a rest. It's someone else's turn to volunteer. I suppose you will be going back to work next week now the summer's over."

"Yes," sighed Jess. "The summer's over..." And a strange sort of holiday romance, she thought, but did not say out loud.

Anna glanced at Jess in an odd way, but much to Jess's relief, said nothing.

Chapter 40

I was born in Glasgow a few years before the war. One of my earliest memories is of some ships on fire on the Clyde. After school, I went on to study engineering, and worked in various factories, looking after the machinery. There weren't all the current health and safety regulations in those days; in some places the working conditions were quite dangerous, so my trade union used to send me under cover to check that the systems were operating properly. I used the name "Berwick Dundee" and until quite recently, I would sometimes get people sidling up to me in the street,

*saying, "Didn't you used to be Berwick Dundee?" In fact, I still use the
name occasionally - I find it can be useful to have an alias!*

*My wife and I married young, she was from an unhappy home background,
and was only sixteen. Of course, people have always been able to marry at
that age in Scotland, (that's why Gretna Green was popular with couples
coming up from England), so her family could not stop us getting hitched.
But she wanted to get away from her family, so straight after the wedding,
we eloped to England - probably the only people to do it that way round... I
had been offered a job working on the new power stations in Yorkshire, so
we moved here. Morag, our daughter was born that first year.*

*Sadly, the marriage broke down, and we divorced. I felt very bad about
this, because my daughter was still very young. My wife remarried, and I
decided I would go to university. I enrolled on a course in sociology. At
that time, there were not so many mature students, and I was with all these
naïve youngsters, who had seen almost nothing of life. This was before gap
years became popular. I could talk about the problems of real working life,
and everyone appreciated my input in the seminars, including the lecturers;
many were ivory tower types who had never had a proper job.*

*By this time, I was becoming involved with CND – they used to be known as
'Ban the Bomb'. I have always been a political animal and a good speaker,
so I was in demand at meetings. There were lots of rallies and marches and
demonstrations against such abominations as Cruise missiles and Trident
submarines. I went to Greenham Common, where the peace women were
camping for years, as a gesture of solidarity, for an open weekend, and as
luck would have it, I met a woman who became my new partner. I've never
found it difficult to get partners, it's easy to pick up like-minded people on
demos and at places like Greenham- the things that went on in those
bushes!*

*Increasingly, I felt bad about having lost touch with my daughter, so I went
back to see if I could find her, but there was no trace of her on the electoral
roll. Of course, she would by then have grown up, probably married and
changed her name, or moved away – anything could have happened in the
intervening years. Then by chance a former work-colleague contacted me;
it turned out that his son lived around the corner from Morag! She was still
in the same town, but had married and had three boys. She was using her*

*married name, which was why I had been unable to find her. It turned out
that I have three grandsons, whose existence I had been completely
unaware of! It has been such a joy, getting to know them. They are all fine
young men.*

*Eventually, my partner left me. I think she wanted someone without my
health problems, once I began having these mini-strokes. I always said that
I wanted to go straight from being fully independent to being dead, and to
miss out this in-between stage where you're dreading drooling into your
bib and being talked to as if you were a child. But it's actually not as bad
as I feared --at least, not in this care home, and not yet. I can still play the
piano after a fashion, and we have sing-songs every Sunday afternoon. I
manage to get round the corner to the library and the pub every day. And
those young Filipina lassies who look after us are all very smiley and
pretty, it does an old man's heart good to see them in the mornings, so I
suppose I really mustn't grumble!*

Chapter 41

Alex clattered in looking rather flushed. "Mum, I'm in a film, but I don't
want to be. Do you know how can I get out of it?"

"What? You'd better explain what's happened!"

"Some geezer's been roaming around Hebden filming drunks and druggies.
I was off my face one night in the street, and he filmed me, although I
really don't remember saying he could. Now some of my friends are saying
they've seen a preview of the film and I'm in it! I got this director guy's
number off a mate and spoke to him, but he says the film's already been
edited and it can't be changed, and that anyway, I agreed to be in it. So
what do you think I should do?"

"Well, it does all sounds rather unethical, taking advantage of people when
they are in no fit state to give informed consent."

Jess tracked down the director on Facebook and sent him a message. He
then rang Jess and confirmed what he had already told Alex, that the film
had been finally edited and it would cost thousands to change it now.

"But can't you just obscure Alex's face or disguise his voice?" asked Jess. The director said he could not, and reiterated that Alex has in fact agreed to appear in the film.

"Yes, but he was obviously drunk at the time! That's not really informed consent. And someone I know who works as an extra tells me directors should always get written consent from people appearing in their films." The director said there was nothing he could do at this late stage, since the film was about to première. He told Jess that there was to be a Question and Answer session after the Hebden Bridge screening, and offered to put Alex on the guest list, if he would care to attend. Alex declined, but |Jess thought she had better go and see just what sort of a state Alex had been in when he was filmed. She bought a ticket, since it seemed that the offer of a guest ticket did not apply to anxious mothers of unwitting participants.

Alex appeared on screen about halfway through the film. He and his mates were sitting in the Square, all apparently rather the worse for wear, when the camera approached. Jess noted that Alex had indeed rushed up to the cameraman, saying that if he was making a film about Hebden Bridge he should realise that there was not much else for people to do except grow cannabis amid the beautiful Pennine scenery. Jess realised that he was being ironic, and in fact Alex's contribution was practically the only moment of light relief in an otherwise almost unremittingly sombre film, which featured several tragic deaths of young people, apparently as a result of taking harmful substances. It was a very hard film to watch, and harder still was the realisation that one of the contributors had actually died during the filming; the film cut from a shot of her happily posing for the camera to a shot of her boyfriend looking at her funeral flowers. Another young man had died since the filming; he had apparently been found under railway arches, and his family was in the cinema audience. If it was hard for Jess to watch, how much harder must it have been for the families of those young people featured who were sadly no longer alive.

When it came to the Q and A session, a number of people made the point that drink and drugs were a problem in many towns, and not just in Hebden Bridge. A variety of theories were put forward, some blaming the hippy culture of the 1970s, the darkness of the Berringden valley in winter, ("Valley Bottom Fever") or lackadaisical parenting. Jess was moved to get to her feet at this last comment. She pointed out that once young people turned eighteen, there was little that parents could do, since their children were now legally adults. The film had concentrated on those aged over 18, and beyond parental control. While Alex had been a young teenager, Jess had striven to control his unruly behaviour, even following him deep into the woods to see where he and his pals had their drinking den, and throwing away any drugs which she came across in her house, be it ecstasy, cannabis, or magic mushrooms, much to Alex's annoyance. Jess also pointed out that her son was now about to go off to university and she hoped he had come through his druggie episode. He had not really wanted to appear in the film or even to see it, since he was trying to make a fresh start and did not want to be reminded of his past mistakes. She sat down after speaking, and the one of the cinema usherettes, a former neighbour, came and put her arm around Jess, assuring her that she was a good mother and had done all should could for both her sons. Jess really appreciated her kind gesture.

Alex was waiting at home. "What's it like? Am I so bad?"

"No, you're OK, a bit merry, but I've seen you much worse. The film is pretty dreary, though. So very sad, all those young deaths – that's what inspired the director to make it, he seemed to be always coming back for funerals. If it raises awareness, maybe it'll do some good in the end - let's hope so!"

The Hebden Bridge screening was by no means the end of the matter, since the film toured various festivals all over the country, and was nominated for a number of awards. The director was interviewed on national television, where the clip featuring Alex was broadcast to the daytime viewing public. However, the first Alex heard of it was when a friend sent him a text asking him if he was aware that he had just appeared on TV. Alex complained to the relevant broadcasting standards authority, because once again, his permission should have been sought before his image was used, and the code of practice had clearly not been observed. After a few weeks, he received an apology from the programme's producer. Jess suggested that he should perhaps have asked for a small sum of money in compensation for hurt feelings, but Alex said he just wanted an end to the sorry affair. However, the film was due out on DVD shortly, and an entirely new audience would be introduced to his drunk and disorderly goings-on, so his wish for the whole thing to simply go away was unlikely to be realised.

"The UK does not have a proper privacy law, and once an image gets into the public domain, there seems to be no stopping anyone from reproducing it, unless of course you're wealthy and can get a super-injunction. I had always imagined that the only people likely to be affected by this would be film stars or footballers or reality show contestants – people who make their living by being in the public eye; I never thought it would be of the slightest concern to people like us," mused Jess. "Famous people are awarded compensation if the courts deem that their privacy has been invaded – look at the phone hacking scandal, people like Sienna Miller received thousands. Of course, they will all have agents to handle their affairs. There's one law for the rich, it seems, and another for the rest of us, law centres are closing through lack of funding, and legal aid is being cut. Although if you had looked on the web you might possibly have found some help..."

"Just want it all to go away, Mum; I don't want to have to talk about it or think about it any more. I wish the film had flopped. I really hope it doesn't get any more awards, and that no-one buys the DVD. Just want to concentrate on getting ready for university now...."

Alex went upstairs to do a bit more packing and Jess took Mash out for a walk. Being of a persistent nature, she would probably have tried to take matters further if it had been up to her, but Alex evidently preferred the ostrich approach. Alex reappeared an hour later, saying that he had to go to Leeds before he left for university, to visit Will in prison.

"He's in Armley again, Mum, been sentenced to twelve months, so no more late-night fish-pie suppers with that poor lad, not now he's behind bars..."

"Why, what's he done?" Jess wondered why the Queen was once again playing the part of Will's landlady.

"Tried to rob a convenience store, look it's all here in the local paper," said Alex, unfolding that week's copy of the 'Hebden Bridge Times'.

Will had apparently stolen two crates of beer worth £15.89. According to the report in the paper, he had threatened the young shop assistant with a steel toe-capped boot and had been caught on the shop's CCTV. Will was already on licence from his previous jail term for shop-lifting, and the court heard that his criminal record was littered with theft and petty offences over several years. He was exactly the same age as Alex, the two had grown up together, and been friends since childhood. Now Alex was about to leave for university. Alex seemed to have come through his earlier trials and tribulations, but Jess knew that there but for the grace of God...

"Why does he do it? There's simply no sense to it! He told me he wanted to go straight for the sake of his child..."

"Sense doesn't come into it, Mum. He's seriously addicted, he's an alkie, he needs help. Let's hope they can do something for him inside, although they didn't manage to sort him out last time. Anyway, I'll go and see him before I leave – it's the least I can do." With that, Alex returned upstairs to prepare for a future so very different from that of his childhood friend.

Chapter 42

It's a going to be rather difficult for me to tell you my story, it's really quite a delicate matter even these days, but I want to do it, so that I know it will be on record somewhere. That door is shut, isn't it, Jess? I'm not sure how much they know in here, the staff and the other residents. They probably think I'm just Tim's friend, although some of them may have guessed the truth. In fact, we were –are- gay partners. That's why I'd prefer not to give my name. I know there's all this Gay Pride these days, people strutting about in fanciful costumes, coming out of the closet; but I belong to a generation which can remember when it was illegal to be homosexual, you could be prosecuted, until after the Wolfenden Report. That was in the 1960s, and until then we really had to be careful - and I'm still careful even now. Not everyone wants to flaunt their sexuality, we're not all bohemian, like Freddie Mercury; but it seems so much worse with Tim's illness, because I can't tell anyone how much I'm hurting.

It all began at boarding school, with crushes on older boys; and really, I've never been interested in women, in that way. I have always got on well with women and have lots of women friends, but I've never wanted a female partner. People sometimes say it's just a phase, which most boys grow out of, but I never did. Most of my school friends got married, it was more or less expected, but some did it to conceal their true sexuality, and felt very

115

guilty about cheating on their wives. I suppose to some people it can all seem rather sordid, the whole Hampstead Heath cottaging scene, but that's the way it was. The revelation of a gay affair or partnership could ruin a man, and it still has the power to make headlines, especially if it involves a politician or a rock star. Look at that Cabinet Minister recently, from a Catholic family; it must have been such a shock for his parents when it all came out. Tim and I met at art college, and we've been together ever since. People who don't really know us think we're simply business partners. We are interior designers. We have a large house, Tim had the ground floor while I lived upstairs - an ideal arrangement. We explained to our families that we had set our hearts on that particular house but couldn't afford it unless we shared. We would holiday in Morocco, or Italy or the South of France, it has been a good life. No children; we thought at one time about adopting, but it all seemed too complicated, too many hoops to jump through. And it would have meant explaining our relationship to officials, and neither of us wanted to do that, we're very private people. Tim was keener on adoption than I was; but he did not pursue the idea, out of loyalty to me.

Now he has this awful illness, and needs so much care. At first, we had the ground floor adapted; the doorways were widened for a wheelchair, the kitchen modified, the bathroom altered etc. But the disease is galloping along, and in the end he wanted to come in here, to save me the worry of caring for him. We could have had a Social Service direct payments budget and employed our own staff - I was all for doing that, but Tim said he didn't want an army of strangers invading our house. He would rather remember our home as it always was, with just the two of us there together. He wanted us to maintain our privacy, as we have done all our lives, not to lose it simply because he was ill.

I can't tell you how wretched I am at the thought of losing him. He has been the love of my life.

Chapter 43

Jess was planning to go to Blackburn with her friend Noreen, to attend a meeting in the Cathedral, where several former Guantanamo Bay prisoners were to speak. However, a hour before they were due to meet, Jess received a call from a distressed Noreen, saying that she would not be able to come as her husband, Sam, had been arrested and there was no-one to look after the three children.

"Arrested? On what charge?"

"We were raided early this morning, there were ten of them, it was awful; the dog ran away in fright. They dragged Sam out onto the street, he was just wearing his underpants, the kids were screaming and crying. The police ransacked the house...." Noreen began to sob. Then she resumed her story. "They were looking for drugs, and they found some prescription drugs..."

"But that's OK if they were prescription drugs, nothing illegal?"

"No, it's still an offence because he did not actually have a prescription for them. He was taking them to help with his health problems. And I think that maybe he was planning to sell them to people, there were a lot of them. The police arrested him and they are holding him until the CP S decides whether they are going to prosecute. So I must stay here with the kids and tidy the house up and wait to see what's happening."

"Is there much damage? And won't the police have to repair it?"
"No they do not have to repair the door because they actually found these drugs. They only have to do the repairs if nothing is found...."

"Oh, Noreen, I am so sorry to hear this," sighed Jess. "How awful for you – and the children. And what about poor Rajah? Has he come back? Would you like me to come up there and wait with you for news?"

"It's OK, Rajah came back when it had all quietened down and went straight to his kennel. Jess, Nick is here now, I asked him to drop by so I won'tt be on my own this evening. Don't worry, I'll be all right now."

Jess was so upset to hear her friend's story that she almost decided not to go to the Blackburn meeting. Then she thought that maybe should after all stick to her plan, since Noreen now had Nick with her, so she went to the station and just managed to catch the train. The cathedral was a short walk from Blackburn railway station, and it was quickly filling up with people. Jess sat down on the end of a row halfway up the aisle, and was soon joined by another middle-aged woman who scurried over to sit in the next seat.

"Don't you feel rather ashamed?" she muttered, leaning over towards Jess.

Jess was not quite sure what the woman was referring to. Of course, the so-called 'war on terror' had been erroneously prosecuted in her name, along with those of all other thousands of anti-war British citizens; and the process of 'extraordinary rendition', and the prison at Guantamano Bay were terrible affronts to human rights. She supposed that must be what the woman meant.

"Of course I do! I never wanted the war. I went on that demo in London in 2003, along with a million others..."

"I don't mean that! Of course, I went on the march, I'm a Quaker, and a whole coach load of us went from our meeting. But just look around, how many other white faces do you see here? Very, very few; it's as though the native British population does not feel that this meeting has any relevance to them, since the speakers are not white."

"Oh, I see what you mean," said Jess, glancing around the by now almost full cathedral. The overwhelming majority of the people attending the event appeared to be from an Asian background, although there was a sprinkling of white people near the back. To her surprise and shock, Jess even fancied that she saw Richard among them, but could not be sure it was him at that distance. She had never received a reply to the voice-mail message she had left for him a week ago; her mother had been absolutely correct, it seemed that men did not want women to contact them, and that those old rules about letting men make the running still applied even after all those years...

Jess forced her mind back to the present. The woman next to her was looking at her expectantly, awaiting her thoughts on the matter of the ethnic composition of the cathedral audience.

"Yet this is something that everyone should be very concerned about. My father was in the First World War, and he was always going on about how he fought to defend our precious British freedoms. Now so many of our basic rights have been suspended, and an innocent young man can be shot dead at an underground station simply for having a dark complexion..."

The meeting was about to begin. Jess was very impressed by the four speakers, who spoke with sincerity and without bitterness of their terrible experiences of interrogation and torture. One of them had written a book which she decided to order from the library. After the talk, she went over to the book stall, and was perusing the book dust-jacket when she became aware of some people passing close by, and recognised Richard's voice.

"We can go back with Alice if you two go in Joe's car. It makes more sense that way."

"OK; and shall we all meet up tomorrow at the 'Fox'?" a woman's voice.

"Great; see you all then!" said Richard. Jess did not feel that it would be appropriate to spring out from behind a pillar and accost him as he was about to leave. He clearly had no intention of contacting her, and anyway she ought to be getting to station, since her train was due in a few minutes.

Jess left by a different exit, so as not to bump into Richard and his friends, and hurried through the chilly streets, just managing to catch her train. She was glad she had made the effort to attend the meeting and hear what the speakers had to say, but found to her annoyance that it had been a little unsettling seeing Richard again. She had told herself over the last few weeks that it was quite for the best that he had not rung her, she was not even sure they would have very much in common, since she had no idea what interested him apart, obviously, from folk music. They had not got around to discussing whether he shared her interests in dogs or writing or barn dancing. They had been so busy with the Koreans that they had not had much time for general chit-chat, and that last day on the boat trip they had been occupied admiring the scenery. Jess had concluded that if she and Richard had been given the opportunity to get to know one other properly, they may not really have liked each other very much, and that it was probably far better in the long run that things had been left as they were.

Chapter 44

Hello, Jess, we wanted to talk to you, because we were missionaries in Africa for many years, and we thought you might like to hear our story. It begins in Oxford where George and I met; that would be in the early 50s.

Yes, our bicycles collided – quite by chance, but I couldn't believe my luck when I saw Iris! That was the luckiest accident I ever had!

George was training for the ministry, and I was training to be a teacher. As soon as we were both qualified, we were sent overseas. All of our four children were born in Africa. It was a wonderful time; we were in a very remote village, but we felt that we were able to help make a difference to the people's lives, I taught at primary school and ran simple healthcare projects, while George went all around the area, preaching and teaching.

I had had the call, and wanted to spread God's word as widely as possible; at the same time, I realised that the people responded to us because we were trying to be practical, and they could see that we were just an ordinary young family. Iris helped the women make mosquito nets to protect the children from malaria. We got a number of old sewing machines sent out from Oxford, people in Britain were going over to electric ones at the time, so we ran an appeal, and collected the hand machines, had them reconditioned and shipped out. We also had a load of netting donated from a factory, to make the mosquito nets. I helped the men dig a well so the villagers could have clean water. Not revolutionary, but very important. And of course, we ministered to their souls, set up a Sunday school, helped nurse the sick, did whatever we could.

Tell Jess about that run-in you had with the local witch-doctor!

Oh yes, he thought we were taking his trade away from him. He used to charge people for his spells and potions, and of course, we would help people for free. For instance, if we thought a woman was anaemic we would take her to the clinic in the nearest town to get some iron tablets, but he would prescribe a traditional remedy and expect payment for it. Sometimes if people were depressed, simply coming to church, talking things through and getting support from friends would be enough to help. So this muti-man came round for a showdown, but he was limping, and it

turned out that he had an in-growing toe-nail; we happened to have some ointment which could help, and we managed to persuade him that we were not in competition, we were complementing his work. And his own mother was a member of our congregation, so she had a few words with him. Oh, there are so many stories we could tell you about our African days, you'd be here all week! But after fourteen years, we had to leave; civil war was just about to break out and it was becoming unsafe for us to stay. We also had both sets of elderly parents back here, needing our assistance, and naturally, we had to consider our own children's education. Of course, it was a wrench, to finally leave after all that time! But we were able to get our parents settled into care, and our children all went to university. They have families of their own, now; we have eleven grandchildren! They live all over the country, but they all visit regularly.

George still helps with the local church, he fills in if the regular minister is away, or if anyone is ill. He's composed several songs using African rhythms, and they've been performed in the church!

Iris ran the church wives' group until last year, when her arthritis got too bad, and we decided to come in here. We're very lucky, we have this lovely big room on the corner, it faces South-West, so we get the afternoon and evening sun, and see it's got a balcony, so Iris can grow a few flowers and herbs in pots.

We still write to people in our African village, and over the years, several have come over to this country to study, so we've been able to have them to stay. We can still do this, at least, for short periods, as there's a guest-room on the ground floor of the main building, which is really handy. And now we can use email to communicate with our friends, which is so much better, because the African post was not always terribly reliable..."

And now we're looking into getting SKYPE, you can talk to people all over the world! And if they have a web-cam, you can see them as you talk. Apparently there are internet cafés in what are otherwise quite isolated villages. It's amazing what you can do nowadays; nowhere is as remote as it was during our time in Africa. The world is shrinking, as they say. And what amazing changes we've seen in our lifetime!

Chapter 45

Jess was on her way to buy some eggs from a stall run by some local children, when she unexpectedly found herself swept up in a village procession. She had completely forgotten that this Sunday was when the restored war memorial was to be unveiled. Jess decided to do without the eggs, and instead participate in the open-air service. It appeared that half the village had turned out, no doubt helped by the fact that it was a warm and sunny autumn afternoon. The procession was led by a brass band, followed by some men dressed in the khaki World War One uniforms of the Manchester Regiment, complete with fixed bayonets. Then came the British Legion, followed by local representatives of the various other uniformed organisations. Next there was a school-children's choir, the Mayor and his consort, some local councillors, and finally anyone else who felt like joining in, including babies in pushchairs and a few dogs. Jess joined the motley throng, and the procession marched over the bridge to the memorial gardens, where the newly-restored statue of a soldier, swathed in blue cloth, was awaiting its ceremonial unveiling.

Kev the Rev, the local vicar, led the service. Jess was rather disappointed that such a large crowd made so little sound during the hymn singing. People were mostly just mouthing the words, their heads buried in their programmes, or standing silently. Community singing must no longer be cool, reflected Jess; for surely almost everyone would know the tune to "Dear Lord and Father of Mankind", since it had recently been voted one of the nation's favourite hymns. Didn't they sing hymns in schools nowadays? Or was it frowned upon to openly express one's Christianity in these times of political correctness? This ceremony was taking place at a war memorial, built to honour people who had fought totalitarianism, and Jess thought that the best tribute anyone could bestow would be to sing out and sing loud, as the soldiers would have done. She recalled that her late father Jack had told her that his love of singing had been fostered during his years of service in the Great War, when he had fought against the Turks in Palestine, and singing had played an important part in keeping up the troops' morale. Jack had gone on to serve in the Home Guard during the Second World War, and he had always told her that he and the ordinary men like him were prepared to fight and die in order to preserve the precious freedoms and independence of the British people. Now Britain was in the European Union, something Jack had been very much against, and its people were continually under surveillance from CCTV cameras. Jess was fairly sure what Jack would have made of all this, and he would not have been very impressed. Times had changed, of course, and so had attitudes, towards Europe, religion, singing and a great deal else.

The renovated stature was unveiled by the daughter of the man who had performed the same duty at the original unveiling in 1922. The hapless soldier statue had had his head removed by vandals some years since, and the temporary replacement head had never looked quite right. Now he was restored to his former dignified glory, looking out over the gardens towards the hills of the Berringden Valley.

After the service, everyone repaired to the church hall, where a few energetic dancers were doing the jitterbug, and wartime economy recipe cakes were rapidly disappearing. By the time Jess arrived the only food remaining was a rather sorry-looking plate of grated carrot sandwiches, and the queue was moving so slowly that Jess thought that her best chance of getting a cup of tea before nightfall would be to run home and come back with a flask. Still, no-one appeared to be complaining, and if they had, someone would probably have quipped that there was a war on, you know...

Jess travelled to Manchester the following evening to attend the première of Evan's new play. Fortunately, on this occasion, Jess was able to stay throughout the entire duration of the play, which was extremely well-written, thought-provoking, and very entertaining, with strong performances from all six cast members. Because of the arrangement of the room, the play was performed in the round, which made prop shifting rather complicated, with each of the cast members required to bring what they needed into the performance area with them at the frequent scene changes. Beds, desks, chairs, mirrors and other assorted paraphernalia all came and went in smooth and rapid succession. Jess sat with Evan's parents on one of the front rows, opposite a couple who looked to her as though they could be the parents of Jude, the young actor playing the schoolboy. After the play had ended, Jess went over to them and congratulated them on Jude's performance. The father looked at her in amazement and asked how she had known they were indeed his parents.

"It was something about the way your wife was watching him. I was sitting directly opposite and thought that she could only be his mother..."

At this, Jude himself appeared, graciously accepting a kiss from his mother, a handshake from his father, and a compliment from Jess. Meanwhile, everyone was hugging Evan and his parents, and when it became known that Jess had once been Evan's babysitter, she was enthusiastically hugged by the cast as well. It seemed to Jess that eventually everyone in the room must have hugged everyone else, and it was high time to find a quick celebratory drink before returning to the station.

Jess ran through the busy streets to catch the hourly train back home to Mash, just as heavy rain-drops were beginning to fall. Jess wondered why she had not thought to bring an umbrella with her on an expedition to Manchester. As she reached the station, a flash of lightening illuminated the city, and a loud clap of thunder sounded as she dashed onto the platform. Jess threw herself onto the waiting train, which pulled away towards the Pennines under a leaden sky. However, by the time the train reached Hebden Bridge the sky had cleared and the evening was fine. Mash greeted Jess with her usual enthusiasm, and Jess wondered, not for the first time, why she had ever wasted time bothering about men in general, or indeed Richard in particular, when there was someone always so very glad to see her and whose trust she knew she could rely on. She quickly fetched Mash's lead, and together they went across to the field for their evening constitutional, under a star-lit sky.

Chapter 46

My name is Ruby, and I'm fifty. I have rheumatoid arthritis, which means I have severe mobility problems. I live in a flat specially designed for wheelchair users, as you can see, it is actually part of the care home complex, but here in the annexe. I manage as much as I can by myself, but the carers check up on me, and of course I can call them if I need to. When I am feeling not too bad, I can make tea and simple meals, because all the surfaces have been designed to be low enough for me reach easily, and the kitchen is fitted out with all these gadgets. But if I am not well, I can ring through and they bring me a meal from the main kitchen.

I try to be as independent as possible, but often it isn't always easy because of the pain. I feel I've missed out on a lot in life, because I've never married or had children. I know some people in my situation do achieve this, but I always felt that I really had enough trouble looking after myself, without having someone else to care for, especially a tiny child. There is a man, he's also a wheelchair user, who I've recently become close to, ever since he moved into the flat next door; but of course, if we were to go on to marry, there would be no question of having children now, as I'm too old.

I had a job in an office for a few years, before I was in this chair; of course, in those days, there were no laws about equality and accessibility, so once I started using the chair, I had to leave. I could not get the wheelchair into the building, because there were no ramps or lifts, and unfortunately, there were no opportunities for working at home from computer terminals like there are these days. It's a different world now.
The disease limits what I do socially as well; I used to play the violin at barn dances, but my finger joints are too painful these days. I still go to the dances to listen to the music, and I've made a lot of friends over the years. I can travel about in my specially adapted car, and if I don't feel well enough to drive it, one of my friends does, so we go to folk festivals all around the country, when my health permits. I try to get to Sidmouth Folk Week every year, that's my main holiday, and I look forward to it.

I'm very excited at the moment, because I'm about to get an assistance dog, they are trained to help with domestic tasks, like loading the washing machine. I've been to meet him, he's really gorgeous, and he already knows lots of commands, so he's going to be a big help. This flat has access to the garden, through the living room patio windows here; and on good days I can take the wheelchair around the corner to the park. If I'm not well, the carers will take him out for me. There is a dog club in the church hall up the road, and we might join that, so he can socialise with other dogs. His name is Rex. We had a dog when I was a child, he was called Chuckles, and he was my best playmate, so it's really given me something to look forward to. The man I told you about earlier jokes that I will soon come to think more of Rex than I do of him, and he may very well be right!

My parents are still alive, but they are both getting on in years now; I'm their only child, and of course, I can't care for them. It's such a big responsibility, being an only child, I tell them, they should move into the main building here, and we could all live close together. I'd like that.

125

Chapter 47

Alex was about to leave for university. After his chequered teenage career he had finally knuckled down to getting some GNVQs and had been accepted onto a course in Plymouth to do Outdoor Pursuits. Both Jess's Yorkshire -born sons had gone to the West Country for higher education.

"It's just the only place that would have me," said Alex. "I really wanted to go to Brighton, but my grades weren't good enough, so Plymouth it is."

Jess has borrowed an old camper-van in order to transport Alex and all his worldly goods to Devon. They were setting off a day early, as they planned to meet up with Tom en route; he was on a cycling tour of North Devon. Alex had arranged accommodation in a house in Mutley Plain, and the landlord had promised to be there to meet them at 4pm on Wednesday.

The van was quickly filling up, since Alex wanted to take his bike, a large table-lamp, an enormous rucksack, his computer, and the dog. Of course, Mash would be returning to Yorkshire with Jess, since the life of a student was unlikely to fit in well with her routine.

They made steady progress, passing Bristol in the early afternoon. Jess was not really sure whereabouts in North Devon Tom would be, he had not planned an exact itinerary, simply saying that he would go wherever fancy took him. Jess was to ring him as they crossed from Somerset into Devon and he would tell her the best place to meet. Jess, aware that the old van would struggle to climb the notoriously steep hills of North Devon, chose the slightly less arduous route via Blackmore Gate She asked Alex to phone Tom, but there was no signal. They rounded a bend, Alex tried again, the signal had reappeared, and there was a message from Tom. He tried to reply, but it seemed that Tom was once more out of signal. Jess began to wonder if they would be able to achieve a rendezvous before dark, when Alex gave a shout.

"That you Tom? Where are you?"

Jess quickly pulled into a lay-by, anxious not to lose the precarious signal. Tom had reached Lynmouth, and was waiting for them by the seafront.

Mash loved the sea, she especially enjoyed chasing the waves. She was about to rush down to the shore when she spied Tom sitting on a bench outside a pub. Mash also loved Tom, and was momentarily torn between greeting him and the lure of the waves. Remembering her manners, she dashed off to bark joyously at Tom before retreating to the shore. Everyone was by this time very hungry, so they bought fish and chips, and ate them by the sea. Walking back up the main street to the car park, Jess recalled that she had last been here on a school field trip in the 1960s.

"It was only fourteen or fifteen years after the dreadful floods of the 1950s here in Lynmouth," said Jess, as they passed the flood memorial building. "We really got around on those field trips; Glastonbury and Wells, Ilfracombe and Combe Martin, Dartmouth and Slapton Sands. We even got as far as Cornwall once. And it wasn't just geography trips, we used to go down to Torquay to see the ballet every year. Then one Easter we went on a camping field trip to Pembrokeshire, but my mum did not really want to let me go, she said it was far too early in the season for camping ....she was quite right, as it turned out, because the boys' tent blew away one stormy night, they sought refuge in the girls' tent, and we all had to come back." Jess sighed wistfully. "Devon was a good place to grow up."

"Surely you can't still miss the West Country that much after living in Yorkshire all these years," said Tom. "Otherwise you'd have come back."

"I never really had the opportunity to come back, but now, with you in Bristol and Alex in Plymouth, I think it might be time to think seriously about retiring to Exeter, then I'd be halfway between you both."

Alex looked shocked. "Mum, you can't leave the Berringden Valley! We want to be able to come back in the holidays! Berringden Brow is our home! Anyway, the dog wouldn't want to move away from the woods."

"I'm sure she'd settle wherever I lived," said Jess, surprised at his outburst.

"No, Mum, I heard on the radio that students don't want to be worrying that anything has changed at home, you're not supposed to redecorate even! Students can't settle into their college courses if their rooms back home are being cleaned or tidied or their stuff thrown out, so don't you even think of it! And as for moving house – you just can't do it."

127

Jess decided to change the subject, and there was in any case a more pressing matter to deal with, since she did not know where they would be sleeping that night.

"Where are we staying? Have you booked anywhere, Tom?"

Tom said he had a map with all the camp-sites listed, and there was one at the top of the hill. "Maybe we should go fairly soon, before it gets dark."

Getting back up the hill was not going to be easy, thought Jess, since as well as everything she and Alex and Mash had brought with them, they now had to accommodate Tom, his bike and the luggage panniers. The boys had to take much of the stuff out of the van and rearrange it around the two bikes, which greatly excited Mash, who was barking all the while. The camper-van was eventually fully loaded, and Jess was driving out of the car park when Alex spotted his table lamp left behind forlornly in the next parking space. He jumped out to retrieve it and they were at last on their way. The heavily laden van's temperature indicator was dangerously close to boiling point as they neared the hilltop, so Jess was obliged to pull over and allow it to cool down before going any further. It was getting late by the time they reached the camp-site, and the reception was all in darkness. There appeared to be no-one about, and Jess was afraid that they might have left it too late to book in. She thought they would have to spend the night wild camping in a field, or parked up in a lay-by. She rang the bell again, and eventually a man appeared from the depths of the building. He looked at them glumly, as if he had been dragged away from his favourite TV programme. Jess apologised for arriving so late, and asked if there were any spare pitches. The man directed them to a field, and said it would be ten pounds. Jess thought that this was a very reasonable charge for three adults, a camper van, a tent and a dog. Tom quickly put up his tent, while Jess brewed some tea and Alex took Mash for a torch-lit evening constitutional in the designated dog-walking area which the proprietor had indicated. Everyone was tired, and they all settled down by ten o'clock. Despite complaining that the top bunk of the camper-van was extremely uncomfortable, Alex fell asleep quickly. Jess could hear his snores, chiming with those of Mash, who was sharing the lower bunk. Then she fell asleep.

Chapter 48

The morning dawned fine, and on looking out of the van window, Jess realised that they had a commanding view of the sea. They did not need to rush, she and Alex were not expected in Plymouth until mid-afternoon. Tom was continuing his cycling tour and planned to visit Woody Bay next so after breakfast they said their goodbyes and went their separate ways.

Across the county from north to south, up hill and down combe, over moorland and through steeply wooded valleys went the camper-van. Alex marvelled at the variety of scenery, saying he had never realised that Devon was so beautiful.

"But you've been to Devon dozens of times!" exclaimed Jess. "We came almost every year when you were little."

"Don't think I've been to this part before, though," said Alex. "Anyway, I can't remember it. Watch out Mum, there's a 'road closed' sign here, the diversion seems to be off to the left."

Jess was obliged to leave the main road and follow a country lane into the wilds. The diversion signs quickly gave up, so that at the next junction she had no idea of the correct route. She pulled over to consult the map. There came a loud rapping on the van window; Alex opened it, and a small party of young people peered in, pointing and smiling and giggling at them.

"Hi, how are you doing?" said Alex. "We're slightly lost. Don't suppose you know which way to Plymouth?" The young people carried on giggling. Jess imagined that perhaps they had never before seen a camper-van so ancient. Then a harassed young man appeared, breathless from running.

"There you all are! I asked you to wait while I paid for the eggs at the farm, but no, off you all went without me. I won't be able to take you out for any more walks if you keep leaving me behind. Oh - can I help you?" he asked Jess. Alex meanwhile, was showing a delighted Mash to the young people, who were taking it in turns to lean through the van window to stroke her.

Jess asked for directions to Hatherleigh, the nearest village of any size, and the young man showed her the correct road to take. Mash and Alex said goodbye to their new friends, and they were on their way once more. The diversion and lack of helpful signs had delayed them somewhat, but they still managed to reach Plymouth by 4 o'clock. Jess found the house where Alex was to meet his landlord, and Alex rang the bell. The man, who said his name was David, welcomed them into the house and offered them tea. He showed them the room Alex was to have, and explained that Alex would be fine there for the first few days, just while he got settled into college, but that next week there was a Colombian MA student coming into the room. Jess and Alex could not believe their ears.

"But we booked this room for Alex! We understood that he could have it for the whole of this academic year."

"Yes, you did, but then this Colombian woman rang up in desperation, and I thought her need was greater than Alex's as she was coming further..."

"But why didn't you let us know? Alex will have to find somewhere else!"

"Oh, don't worry, there's probably still a few rooms left; he can try the agencies," shrugged David. "Now, if you can just pay the week's rent..."

But Jess was determined that David was not going to have a penny piece of either her or Alex's money. "Seeing he's been so badly let down, we'd better go and find him somewhere else immediately," said Jess. "And I shall be taking this up with the university, since you are on their approved accommodation list, but I really don't approve of the shabby way you have treated Alex!"

They left David's house and retreated to the van. "Mum, what on earth do we do now?" asked Alex. He looked very shocked. "The agencies will want huge deposits up-front, and parental bond guarantees..."

"Don't worry, we'll find something," said Jess, with more confidence than she actually felt. It was tea-time on a sweltering autumn afternoon in a strange city, but she had no intention of leaving Plymouth until she had found Alex somewhere to lay his head. Her first thought was that they should both put more credit on their mobile phones, so they walked around the corner to a parade of shops. Alex went into the newsagent, while Jess and Mash waited outside. The shop window was full of advertisements for accommodation, and Jess began writing them down. She noted that most of the contacts were mobile phone numbers, but there was one rather faded postcard at the bottom of the window, advertising bed-sits, which gave a number with the Plymouth area code. Jess dialled the number and spoke to a lady, who explained that the postcard had been there for several weeks, and she had actually asked the newsagent to remove it, because the bed-sits were all now let, and there was only one tiny box- room left.

"May we see it?" asked Jess. "We've come from Yorkshire, and my son has been let down by the man we booked with, so he has nowhere to stay."

"You mean he needs somewhere tonight?" queried the lady. "Oh dear, I haven't had a chance to vac and dust. Does he have his own bedding?"

"Yes, he has all he needs, and we really would like to see the room, no matter what condition it's in," said Jess. "He can help you clean it up."

Alex meanwhile, had emerged from the shop, so Jess indicated that he should speak to the lady with the small room, and handed him her phone. The address given was not far away, so armed with the street map which Alex had thoughtfully bought at the newsagent's, Jess drove the van around at the appointed time. The house was a large double-fronted villa on a leafy avenue, but it appeared to be somewhat run down, with flaking paint and peeling stucco, and a wilderness of a front garden. As Jess rang the doorbell, she could hear the jangling sound echo down a hall. The door creaked loudly when it was eventually opened by a short stout man wearing dark glasses, who introduced himself as Mr. Mervyn Sanders.

"Good evening, I hope this is a convenient time," said Jess. "This is Alex."

Alex shook hands with Mr. Sanders. Mash could be heard barking from the van, and Alex called to her to be quiet.

"You'm got a dawg withee?" enquired Mr. Sanders. "Well, bring un in!"

"Are you sure your wife won't mind?" asked Jess.

"Of course 'er won't mind! 'Ere, Patty, they've brung their dawg with 'em. Us loves dawgs, don' us! What sort be 'un? A Staffy? Patty and me loves Staffies! Let un off 'er lead! Bring un 'ere! Lemme stroke 'un!"

Alex released Mash from the van, and there followed several minutes of chaos, as Mash rushed down the garden path and through the hall, to greet a smiling Mrs. Sanders, who was stationed in the kitchen doorway with a ginger biscuit at the ready. She then dashed back to bark delightedly at Mr. Sanders, before charging into the living room, where she flopped down contentedly onto a multi-coloured crocheted blanket on the sofa. Mr. Sanders sat down next to her, whereupon she flung herself onto his lap and began licking his face. Jess was afraid for his dark glasses, but Mr. Sanders did not appear in the least to mind Mash's enthusiasm, in fact he appeared to be almost as delighted as she was.

"Welcome home, Alex," murmured Jess.

Soon they were all sitting in the living-room, drinking tea and watching a huge flat screen television. It was almost like being at the cinema, thought Jess, and its newness contrasted sharply with the rest of the furnishings. Mrs. Sanders explained that they had bought the largest TV set available because of Mr. Sanders' failing eyesight. Presently Mrs. Sanders said that they should go and see the box-room, and Alex should bring his things in from the van, assuming he wanted to stay.

"I definitely want to stay!" said Alex. "I'm just so glad that card was still in the newsagent's window."

Jess said that she ought to take Mash for a walk around the block, and Mr. Sanders said he was off for a walk on Dartmoor. Jess looked surprised.

"He always goes about this time," said Mrs. Sanders. "He catches the bus up to Yelverton and walks around there for a bit before dark."

"May I use the bathroom?" asked Jess. Mrs. Sanders indicated a small room with a high ceiling and dingy lino just off the hall. It was some years since Jess had used a pull-the-chain style flush or hard toilet paper, and she recalled both these had featured in the bathroom of her childhood home.

By the time Jess and Mash had returned from their walk, Alex had moved all his stuff into the little room, which was now completely full. His bike was in the shed at the back. The rent was £50 per week, with a fortnight payable in advance. Mrs. Sanders explained that people were coming and going in the house all the time, many of her lodgers were foreign students on short language courses, so Alex could move into a bedsit as soon as one became available, if he needed more space. However, if he wanted to move somewhere else entirely, she would require only a week's notice. To Jess's relief, here was no parental guarantee or enormous deposit to find. The Sanders family appeared to operate on trust.

Jess and Mash were preparing to say their goodbyes when Mr. Sanders suddenly reappeared, fresh from his walk on Dartmoor. He was still wearing his dark glasses, and carrying a white stick and a Thermos flask.

"And where be you and the dawg stayin' tonight?" he asked. Jess explained that she was going to sleep in the camper-van. She would drive out to the edge of the city and look for a camp-site, or a quiet lay-by.

"But you can stay here!" exclaimed Mrs. Sanders. "Our front bedroom is free just now, those French language girls aren't coming in til next week."

"Are you sure?" asked Jess. "There's Mash as well remember..."

By this time, Mr. Sanders was conducting her to the front of the house. He opened the door to a large room with pink wallpaper, pink curtains and a pink carpet, with pink quilts on the twin beds and a lamp with a pink shade on the bedside table.

"Be our guest! "You and the dawg 'll be in the pink in 'ere" he insisted. Jess thanked him profusely, then went to fetch her sponge bag and Mash's blanket. It was getting dark now, and the evening was starting to feel rather chilly. Jess collected her things, then locked up the camper-van and thankfully opened the creaking house door. Mrs. Sanders was making more tea, Alex and Mr. Sanders were playing dominoes, and Mash was asleep by the fire. Jess was suddenly glad that David the two-timing landlord had re-let his room to the Colombian MA student. She was quite sure that Alex would be happy here.

Chapter 49

Jess and Mash returned home from the West Country to a quiet house. Contrary to Alex's instructions, Jess had plans to redecorate his room, which was looking decidedly shabby. Jess thought it seemed strange for her even to be able to get through the bedroom door, now that Alex had taken so much away with him to Plymouth and the floor was no longer littered with empty beer cans, bottles, and a medley of old jeans and discarded pants and socks. Jess had asked Mark from around the corner to do the decorating, since she did not want to risk becoming dizzy and falling off a step-ladder; however, there was still a certain amount of preparation to be done before Mark could start painting. Jess stripped the bed and tidied away some old papers. She fetched a broom and knocked down several cobwebs, then put a dust-sheet over the bookcase and rolled back the carpet. She had already bought the paint, so Mark could start the decorating any time it suited him. Jess collected up a large black bag of rubbish and took them out to her bin. To her surprise, the bin was almost full of someone else's rubbish in large green bags. How annoying, thought Jess. She had also brought an enormous stuffed dog down from the attic; the boys had played with it when they were little, so boisterously that the stuffing was leaking from its seams, and it had definitely outlived its usefulness. There was not room for it in the bin now that someone else had so inconsiderately filled it with their rubbish, so Jess removed the green bags and replaced them with the bedraggled stuffed dog. She left the green bags beside the bin and returned indoors.

How quickly the autumn is going, thought Jess, as she and Mash set out for the woods on their usual Sunday afternoon walk. The clocks had gone back, the leaves had almost all turned colour, and many were now falling; and it seemed that the days were racing by. However, the winter would bring its compensations, since Tom and Alex would be home for Christmas. Jess hoped it would not be too cold a winter. Last year the water pipes had all frozen so she had been obliged to fetch buckets of water from next door.

Meanwhile, she had several talks scheduled over the coming weeks, and hoped to sell a good number of her books before Christmas. Accordingly, she set off to speak to a Probus club at Cleckhuddersfax. Jess had always thought that Probus clubs sounded as though they were groups in favour of public transport, but when she had embarked on her career as a public speaker, she had quickly discovered that they consisted of mainly elderly retired professional and businessmen, or sometimes businesswomen.

The meeting was to be held in a Sports centre on Tuesday morning, and Jess was amused to discover that there was a salsa class, dancing to loud Caribbean music, in an adjoining room, so that she would have to wait to begin her talk until after this had ended. The gentlemen were mostly drinking coffee and chatting, although a few looked as though they were settling down for a snooze as soon as the music ended. Jess had found that this was often a problem with such talks; many men seemed glad of the opportunity for an undisturbed nap, safe amongst friends and well away from their wives. However, afternoon clubs were the worst, since the temptation to sleep after the mid-day meal frequently proved completely irresistible, so that Jess had abandoned giving talks to Darby and Joan or lunch clubs, where her voice had to compete with the sounds of snoring.

Jess had refined her talk to include fewer readings and more funny anecdotes, which audiences seemed to appreciate. She was invariably introduced by Probus Chairmen as a 'young lady, come to give a talk', since although now in her early fifties, she was always younger than her audience. This group were surprisingly responsive, and chuckled in all the right places. At the end, Jess reminded them that their good ladies would no doubt be delighted to receive a small Christmas gift which they had not bought themselves, and amid much laughter, the gents all got up and formed an orderly queue. In a few cases, Jess observed men waking their neighbours, to tell them the meeting and there were amusing books on sale.

"Ho ho, that talk was very good, I'll take a book for my wife; she'll enjoy it and who knows, I might even read it myself!" exclaimed one gentleman.

The Chairman wanted a book but had no money on him, so would Jess trust him to send her a cheque? Jess said she would. These Probus gentlemen were invariably trustworthy types, although she did recall one occasion when a Townswomen's Guild member had simply wandered off with a book; Jess had been busy signing copies and had not realised that she was one book short until she was counting them back into the box. However, the culprit had later telephoned to apologise for her absent-mindedness, saying that it was not until she had arrived home and discovered the book in her shopping bag that she realised she had not paid for it, and a cheque would follow forthwith. She was as good as her word.

Jess was just preparing tea when she heard a scream from the back yard and rushed out to see what was the matter. Kate was standing there, another green rubbish bag on the ground beside her, looking quite shaken.

"There's an enormous dog in your bin! It gave me such a shock! Really, Jess, you ought to warn people!"

"But I didn't know anyone else would see it! What are you doing, looking in my bin, anyway?"

"I'm trying to dispose of some rubbish, and my bin is full up, of course, there are two of us so we create more rubbish, so I really didn't expect your bin to be so full, Jess, what with you being single! How on earth do you manage to fill it when there's only you at home now? Of course, I know we are all meant to re-cycle these days, but Adrian always says he's far too busy to sort out cans and bottles and such-like. I would have thought you had plenty of time for re-cycling though, now Alex has gone!"

Jess was about to explain about clearing out Alex's room, but decided there was no need to justify the contents of her bin to Kate or anyone else.

"Kate, please take your rubbish away, I really don't want it in my yard."

"But what am I supposed to do with it? My bin is full up! Maybe if we squashed your rubbish down a bit and you took this dog thing out..."

But by now, Jess was coming close to losing her temper. She threw Kate's rubbish bags over the wall and shooed a surprised Kate out of her yard.

"Well, Jess, this really isn't very neighbourly of you. That's the last time I give you anything, and you know you've always had first refusal...."

"Good, I don't want anything of yours; I'm trying to cut down on clutter!"

Jess stomped back indoors but found that she had no patience for food preparation, and decided to treat herself to a take-away instead.

Chapter 50

Jess had one final interview to do for the life history project before she wrote up the results. This interviewee was actually living in a care home across the border in Lancashire, but on reading about the project in an academic publication he had sent a request to meet Jess because he wanted his views on care home living recorded. Jess soon got lost, she had taken a wrong turning and blundered onto a labyrinthine semi-derelict housing estate, finding herself driving along dismal streets of boarded up empty houses. Occasionally someone would scuttle by, perhaps a veiled woman, clutching the hand of a small child; or an old man leaning heavily on a stick. Jess could not imagine where they could possibly be going, since there appeared to be no shops, schools, libraries or community centres left in the vicinity. She was finding it impossible to locate the exit. All the streets seemed to lead her back to a dreary grassed area in the centre, sadly overgrown and littered with abandoned fridges, bin-bags and old car tyres. Then Jess noticed a street bordering the grassed area where all the houses were newly rendered, with brightly painted front doors, neatly tended gardens, and satellite dishes. So there was hope for the area after all and here was a corner shop! Jess went in to ask for directions, and the helpful shop-keeper told her how to get back to the Todmorden Road. Jess rang to explain that she was running late, and was assured that the staff would let Jim know she was on her way.

My name is James Brown, and I am 80 years old, a retired GP. You notice that I have told you my surname; I like to be called Dr. Brown, but in here it's all 'Jim'. I don't think it shows much respect, to be called by one's nickname or even a Christian name, but no-one else seems to care. I asked them to use my surname and title, but they don't take any notice, it's like fighting the advancing tide, all this informality. The doctor's receptionists, people at the hospital, the ambulance staff - why, even the vicar calls me 'Jimmy' when he comes to give me communion. I hate being in this place, I'm here very much against my will. They told me that if I did not agree to going into a care home, they would have me sectioned! Can you believe it? They took away my three beloved cats, Pip, Squeak and Wilfred, and stuck me in here, because it was more convenient for my girlfriend Dora. I had no say in the matter! I met her when I was guest lecturing on a cruise ship, talking about naval history, that's my subject. I fell into her clutches, so to speak. She was doing ballroom dancing demonstrations with her gay dance partner, but he had plans to retire and emigrate to California, so she was looking for a new opportunity. You are lucky to catch me on my own today, because she comes most days and sits watching television, endlessly. I often want to put the radio on, or read, but she follows all these daytime soaps. However - I think I've managed to put a stop to all that! Last night, after she left to go home, I pulled out the aerial and ran over it with my electric wheelchair, so the connection is damaged. She'll have to go down to the sitting room with all the old dears to watch TV, and leave me in peace.

I don't really want to tell you about my past, that's private; but you are welcome to record what I think about my life here, and I'll try to keep the language clean! Let it serve as a warning to other men - don't fall prey to a determined woman! What people don't realise is that when you come into one of these places you lose absolutely all control over your life. They say 'It's not a prison', but that's exactly what it is. You can't choose when to have your meals, what to eat, when to get up; they don't like you wearing your dressing gown all day, which is something I often did when I was at home. Your clothes are not your own – I'm quite tall, and look at these trousers! They're obviously not mine, they're far too short - at half mast like this, it's disgraceful; mine have gone lost in the laundry, the name-tag must have dropped off. And I'm sure that man across the corridor has got my new green shirt. Have you noticed how stuffy this room is? The window won't open more than a crack, because of bloody 'health and safety', and I love fresh air. I would like to go into the garden more often, but I can't take my wheelchair in the lift without assistance and they're always too busy to go with me. I've told you about Dora, she never wants to go out, says it's too cold. She gets cross if I have any other visitors, she hates it when my son comes to see me, he lives in Gloucestershire and can't come often. They're always trying to get me join in activities, but I keep telling them, I don't want to play bingo, or do community singing, or craft work. I just want to be left alone! Is that too much to ask? Occasionally, I'll I try to have a conversation with another resident, but I can't understand the local accent, and they always say "You're not from round here are you…" You sound like you're not from round here, either – West Country, I should say. I'm right? A fellow exile in this benighted part of the country. I would love to escape, in fact I've got a plan. The next time they take me to hospital for a check-up, I'll hide a knife in my pocket and hi-jack the ambulance, and tell them to take me to Cheltenham, away from Dora and Yorkshire and bingo and craft work and this poky room. I'd die happy there!

Chapter 51

Throughout the autumn Jess was kept busy transcribing the life story interviews and giving talks. Alex sent her an occasional text message; he said that he was fine, enjoying the caving and climbing and canoeing and other outdoor activities, although he was struggling a bit with the written assignments. He had now moved from the small room into one of the Sanders' bedsits, so had more space and could do his own cooking. Could Jess please text him the recipe for fruit crumble, as he had spotted an abandoned over-grown orchard full of apples and damsons while out on a cycle ride, and was planning to return with his rucksack, since it seemed a pity to waste all that fruit. Mrs. Sanders had said she would like some of it to make jam, which she would share with him, so it did not seem that he would be going hungry, and of course, there was always the supermarket skipping, which was proving very useful in eking out the student loan...

Jess was due to give a talk to a Women's Institute in a remote moorland village. The meeting started as usual with the usual singing of 'Jerusalem' accompanied by a rather inept lady on an out-of-tune piano. The President explained that the usual pianist was unfortunately away. Jess reflected that she must have heard scores of renditions of 'Jerusalem', although she had discovered that a few more modern WIs with a core of younger members actually began their meeting with a glass of wine rather than an anthem. However, no matter what sort of audience she was addressing, men or women or mixed, retired or still working, church groups, business people or social clubs, Jess had found that the questions they asked after the talk were all curiously similar. "How long does it take you to write a book?" "Where do you get your inspiration?" "Do you use a computer?" "How many copies have you sold?" "Have you made much money from your writing?" "How can I publish my story?"

Jess's least favourite question was generally from some clever person at the back, "Do you consider yourself to be the next J.K. Rowling?" this was usually accompanied by giggles or guffaws from other audience members. Jess always replied politely, and tried to inject a little humour into her replies. No, she did not consider herself to be the next anyone, since she was the first and only Jess Greenwood! And nor did she write fantasy, so she was in no way trying to emulate the creator of Harry Potter. Her stories were much more down to earth, no flying involved, and their chief selling point was the fact that people identified with the characters. Jess had lost count of the number of women who had come up to her after her talks and told her that it was as if she had been spying on them, since the incidents she described, or something very similar, had actually happened to them! Problems with teenage children, misunderstandings with men, incidents in supermarkets, strange job interviews, odd conversations overheard in bus queues, things you thought could not possibly be true but it turned out actually were, truth stranger than fiction - such was the stuff of Jess's writing. She wrote about what she knew, and her readership recognised this, so that her quirky stories struck a chord with middle-aged women.

Unfortunately, by the time the kind ladies had made tea and looked at the books, (some even buying them, since Christmas was fast approaching,) Jess was quite late leaving the village hall, and a thick mist had settled on the moors. Jess soon realised that she missed her turning, and was now lost. She did not have a Sat-Nav device, so pulled over onto the grass to consult the map. She switched on the car's interior light, but it was really not that bright, so Jess found a torch in the glove compartment and used that. Just as she was peering at the road atlas, she became aware of fog-lights approaching along the lane. A vehicle stopped and pulled up on the verge behind Jess. The driver might be an axe murderer, thought Jess, but I'll take a chance that he's not and ask if he knows the way back home. Jess leapt out of her car to ask the driver for directions. The driver of the vehicle – a Range Rover - wound down the window, and smiled pleasantly at Jess.

"Can I help you? I noticed that you were looking at the map – and it's really not much of a night for being lost, is it!"

Jess explained that she was trying to find her way back to Berringden Brow. The man nodded and told her that she had come several miles out of her way, and the next turning was a couple more miles up the road, to the right.

"I'm going that way myself – follow me!" he said, again flashing a charming smile. Jess thanked him and returned to her car. She had the feeling that somehow she knew this man, although she could not think how or where they might have previously met. She kept close to the tail-lights of the Range Rover, which eventually signalled that they were about to turn right. Down off the moor they went, following a winding narrow lane between dry-stone walls. At one point the Range Rover came to a sudden halt, the driver jumped out and disappeared in front of his vehicle; Jess heard a sheep bleating as the man shooed it back into a field. Eventually, the mist started to thin, and Jess could just make out the dim lights of civilisation far below. The Range Rover pulled over at a junction, and the driver got out and came over to Jess.

"You know where you are now? Keep straight on and then left at the crossroads, that's the top of the valley road. I'm turning off now, but I'm sure you'll be OK from here."

"I'll be fine, Thank you so much!" said Jess gratefully. The man favoured her with another dazzling smile, and returned to his vehicle. Jess pulled out to pass him, and he waved at her. It was only as Jess was waving back that she realised just where she had seen him before – in the car-park of the care-home, when Anna was asking him for the money to buy May's winceyette nightdresses. Jess's kind moorland saviour was John the con-man, now living the good life on a hill-top farm with his new lady-friend.

Back at home, Jess found Mash awaiting her evening constitutional, and a message on the answer machine from Tom, reporting that the offer he had put in for the re-possessed murder-scene house had not been accepted. Jess realised that she was quite relieved to hear this. There would no doubt be other suitable houses on the market, without such a tragic back-story. She rang Tom back, but it was not an especially convenient time, since Tom was in the process of making cinder toffee, and had added too much bicarbonate of soda to the mixture, which was now effervescing violently.

"Hang on, let me put this stuff outside before it goes all over the floor!" Tom dropped the phone, and Jess could hear the banging of doors and the clattering of tins. Tom returned. "That's better, I've put it on the garden wall. Now what were you saying? You got lost on the moors? Oh no, did you hear that noise?" Jess had indeed heard a loud crash, followed by an agonised miaow. "Ted's in the toffee – I'll ring you back."

It was a further hour before Tom rang. Ted kitten had jumped off the shed roof and into the cooling tins, so that Tom had been obliged to spend half an hour picking congealing toffee out of Ted's fur. Then he had had to pick Ted's fur out of the toffee. Tom, Ted and Jess had all had an eventful night.

Chapter 52

Sehlile and Mia were coming from Leeds to spend the afternoon in Hebden Bridge. Mia loved the children's playground, and Sehlile always liked looking around the shops. Hebden Bridge had fought determinedly to maintain its independent, quirky range of shops, so was unlike the run-of-the- mill high streets of many other British town centres, where all the shops seemed very similar, if not identical, to those found elsewhere.

Jess met her friends at the station, and they set off for the park. It was a bright sunny winter's day, and the playground was full of children and parents. There was a small drama when Mia got stuck on the stairway of the helter-skelter, and could go neither up nor down. Jess was not tall enough to reach her, and neither was Sehlile, so Jess had to shout for a tall person to assist. Mia was almost in tears, and some of the other children were complaining that they could not get past her, while others were queuing patiently. One of the fathers of the other children eventually came over and managed to lift Mia down from her perch. Then Mia climbed onto the model boat; she wanted to steer it, and imperiously waved away the little girl presently holding the steering-wheel, who happened to be Daisy, one of Jess's neighbours. Jess apologised to Daisy and her father, but Daisy kindly relinquished the steering-wheel in favour of Mia.

"You must learn to take your turn," Jess told Mia, wondering how many years it could be since she had said the same thing to Alex. Sehlile was on her mobile phone, so Jess felt herself to be temporarily in *loco parentis*. Then Mia suddenly jumped down from the model boat, she had spied a free swing, and rushed over to it. Jess could scarcely keep up.

"Push me harder" commanded Mia. Jess explained that if she swung her legs to and fro, Mia would be able to swing herself, but Mia did not wish to do this when she had Jess on hand to push. This must be what it's like to have a grandchild, thought Jess. It was a long time since she had spent the afternoon in a children's playground.

Finally, Mia had had enough of playing and requested an ice-cream. Jess took this as their cue to leave, so they crossed the canal bridge and headed towards the shopping area. There was a narrow-boat going through the lock, a sight which Mia had not seen before, so they watched it until it had safely gone through. Jess explained the mechanism to Mia. Hebden Bridge is often full of dogs of all shapes, sizes, colours, breeds and levels of obedience, and Mia was rather nervous of those running around off the lead, so Jess held her hand and explained that the dogs did not want to hurt her, just to be friendly. One of the free-range dogs licked Mia's leg, causing a startled cry. Jess had decided to leave Mash at home, since she disliked crowds, and anyway, Mia would probably have jumped straight back on the train if Jess had brought Mash to meet her.

They found a café, where Jess and Sehlile had tea and Mia had the promised ice-cream. They sat at an outside table and listened to a busker playing his violin – rather well, Jess thought, as she gave him some change. Then they looked in the charity shops, where Sehlile bought a handbag and Jess bought a small pink beaded bag for Mia and a jumper for Alex, who had sent a text asking her to send more warm clothing, as the weather was turning surprisingly chilly, even in Plymouth.

"To think that Alex is now at university!" exclaimed Sehlile. In her mind, Alex would always be the eleven year old boy she had helped a distraught Jess find when he was lost on the streets of Bulawayo all those years ago, for that was how the two women had met. Then Nick emerged from the betting shop, looking understandably pleased with himself, since his chosen horses had all romped home. He stopped to chat with Sehlile, but Mia quickly became bored with all the standing around exchanging pleasantries, and demanded the toilet. Jess took her down to the Trades Club, where she was a member, and so could use their toilets for free, whereas it was necessary to pay to use the council ones. Children were allowed in the club on weekend afternoons, and so were dogs, but it was all rather strange for Mia. She climbed the stairs slowly, tightly holding Jess's hand, shrinking as a Staffordshire Bull terrier cross and his owner went by, sniffing the smell of the exotic Tibetan food as they passed the kitchen, listening to an indie-band act doing their sound-checks in the concert room and secretly wondering just what sort of a place her godmother had brought her to.....

Eventually, it was time for them to head for the railway station so that Sehlile and Mia could get the tea-time train back to Leeds. They found there was quite a commotion, with several buses pulling into the forecourt and crowds of confused people milling around. The ticket office attendant was looking extremely harassed, urging everyone to keep quiet and listen to the tannoy announcements; these related to an incident on the line at Todmorden. It seemed that trains to and from Manchester could not get through, but another train was due in from Leeds shortly, which would then turn back to form the tea-time train. So Sehlile and Mia would be able to travel home as planned, unlike passengers for Manchester, who were being advised to use the replacement buses which had only just arrived.

Jess waited on the platform with her friends for the train from Leeds to pull in. Things were now settling down, since the Manchester passengers were leaving the station building and assembling in the forecourt to board to buses. Just then Sehlile grabbed Jess's arm and pointed across the track to where a man with longish hair was wheeling a bike along the platform.

"That man over there – isn't he the one I saw you with in Devon?"

"Who? Where? Surely you don't mean Richard?" Jess looked across, but the man had disappeared down the ramp. Jess realised that he would soon emerge from the tunnel and up the steps right next to where she was standing. Sure enough, Richard came up the steps, wearing a garish mud-bespattered Lycra outfit, and carrying a bicycle over his shoulder.

"Jess! Fancy seeing you here! Oh, of course, you live near here don't you... what a nuisance this is, I don't know how I'm getting home. I can get on one of the replacement buses, but they won't take bikes. I've been for a ride from home over the moors and all around Haworth and I can't cycle back to Manchester - I've no lights and it's getting dark. I'm not sure what to do..."

"Oh dear, how awkward. There are some cycle lockers outside, maybe you could leave your bike in one of those," said Jess.

"I haven't got a padlock on me, and anyway, I don't really want to leave it here, I'd have to come back and fetch it tomorrow, which would be a drag."

As Richard was speaking, the train from Leeds drew in, there were only two coaches and rather too many people waiting to get on it, so there was a scramble to board. Jess watched anxiously as Sehlile and Mia found the last seats and waved as the train pulled out. Turning around, she found Richard engaged in earnest conversation with the station ticket seller.

"No, it's no use, I asked if I could wait for a later bus which may not be full and put the bike on that, but he said it was against health and safety rules."

Jess noticed how tired he looked, really no wonder after his long cycle-ride.

"Well, I suppose you could always come back to my house and wait there, perhaps have some food, and check with the station in an hour or so, to see if the trains are likely to be running again later on...."

"Could I? Thanks, Jess, that would be great. What shall we do, shall I cycle to your house, or will we be able to squeeze the bike into your car?"

"You can't cycle any distance without lights; if we fold the back seat down the bike will probably go in, I've had Alex's bike in the boot before now, although he did take the wheels off. Do you happen to have a spanner?"

Richard produced a spanner from the bike's saddlebag and removed the front wheel. Somehow they managed to get Richard's bike stowed safely into the car boot, and drove back to Jess's house. Jess unlocked the door and invited Richard in. Richard flopped down onto the sofa and sighed with relief, while Jess went into the kitchen to make some tea. Mash, alerted by the sound of voices to the presence of a stranger, came downstairs with her tail furiously wagging, and launched herself onto Richard's lap. Luckily, he liked dogs, and was happy to make a fuss of her, much to Mash's delight.

"What an amazing stroke of luck, bumping into you like that, Jess! I've thought about you so often since the summer, and you must be wondering why I didn't call you, like I said I would, but I lost my phone, which had your number saved in the address book, and I hadn't kept a separate record of it, so there was no way of getting in touch with you. I am sorry."

Jess handed Richard his tea. Over the years, various men had come up with a variety of excuses for not phoning her, the most common of which was that they had lost her phone number. Jess had wryly come to believe that hers must be the most easily lost number on the planet. However, losing the phone did sound fairly plausible, and people didn't often write numbers down in a paper address book these days, they simply relied on their mobile phone's built-in contact list. And of course, when she had tried to call him it had gone straight to voice mail because his phone was lost, and she had left a message which, unbeknown to her, would not be retrieved and therefore could not possibly be returned, leaving her to draw the wrong conclusion.

Richard drank his tea and stretched out on the sofa, with his long legs draped over the end, since it was only a two-seater and rather too small for him to lie comfortably. He reached for his phone to check a text message, and Jess noted was not the same model as the one she had seen him with in Devon, but something rather more up-to-date looking. Jess's thoughts were now turning to supper; she had planned to have some left-over tuna bake, which she supposed might stretch to two portions if she did some potatoes to go with it, and there were a few salad things in the fridge. But before she got on with any cooking, there was something she felt she must say.

"I saw you, in Blackburn cathedral, at the Guantanamo prisoners talk."

"You saw me there? Why on earth didn't you come over and say hello?"

"Well, you were with a group of friends, and I didn't want to intrude. And since you hadn't phoned, I thought it was best to leave things as they were."

"Jess, this is absurd! I really wanted to get in touch with you, I even rang the organisers of the Combe Salterton festival to ask for your number, but they said it would be against their strict confidentiality policy to give out people's contact details. Then I searched for you on Facebook, but there are so many Jess Greenwoods listed, and none of them looked anything like you. And you actually saw me, and didn't feel that you could even come over and speak to me...I can't get over that! I thought we were friends...."

"Yes, I thought so too; but when you didn't phone, or respond to the voice message I left for you, I thought differently." Jess was indeed on Facebook, but instead of posting a picture of herself, she had used one of Mash; lots of people put pictures of their pets, and of course, Richard had not met Mash until half an hour ago, so would not have known that this was her account.

Jess and Richard looked at each other without speaking. Mash continued to wag her tail and then began to lick Richard's bare leg in an effort to gain his attention. His Lycra cycling outfit extended to below his knee, and his lower leg was proving much too enticing for Mash. Jess lit the fire, then dragged Mash away from Richard and settled her on the hearthrug.

"Right, I'll get supper started, and maybe you'd like to have a shower?" said Jess briskly. It made no sense to dwell on ifs and whys and why-nots.

"Well, that would be really great, but I haven't got any other clothes to change into, and these are rather disgusting....oh dear, I seem to have managed to get mud on your sofa..."

"Oh, don't worry, it will brush off. And I expect I can find you some clean clothes; Alex left some of his stuff behind when he went to Plymouth, I think you and he are about the same build. Let me see what I can find."

Jess went up to the attic, and rummaged in the depths of Alex's cupboard. She emerged with an old T-shirt and a pair of new underpants still in the packet, which she had put it in last year's Christmas stocking and Alex must have forgotten about. There was also a pair of track-suit bottoms which Alex no longer wore, and of course the Oxfam jumper she had bought only today. She gave these to Richard and also provided him with a clean towel.

Richard came down from the bathroom wearing Alex's clothes, with his long hair all tousled and wet and a beaming smile on his face.

"Thanks, Jess that feels so much better."

"Good," murmured Jess, serving up the supper. "Oh, while you were upstairs, I rang the train enquiries and they said the line to Manchester will be re-opening in about an hour and a half, so you should be able to get home OK. I'll run you back to the station later on."

"That's very kind of you, Jess. I really appreciate it. And I'll make sure I get Alex's clothes back to you next week - don't let me leave without putting your number in my new phone. I'll write it in my diary as well."

They ate their supper, and then Jess made a fresh pot of tea. Richard looked exhausted, he was yawning and he could scarcely keep his eyes open.

"You'll be OK for a few minutes while I take Mash across the road for her evening walk? Help yourself to more tea, if you'd like some, there's plenty in the pot," said Jess, fetching Mash's lead and flashing collar light. Richard nodded and smiled wearily, then lay back on the inadequate sofa.

Mash did not want to stay out long, not when there was a fascinating man at home whom she felt had not yet paid her sufficient attention. So they returned after ten minutes, to find the living room empty. Mash barked in surprise. Jess assumed that Richard must be in the bathroom, but when he did not re-appear after a while, Jess went to find out where he was. Her bedroom door was ajar, and there she found her exhausted guest, stretched out on top on the bed, fast asleep. Jess did not have the heart to wake him, so she fetched a spare blanket from the airing cupboard and placed it over his recumbent body, then returned quietly downstairs to do the washing-up. Later, Jess rang the train enquiry number and found that contrary to earlier predictions, the line to Manchester was still closed and unlikely to re-open for several hours. There was no point in waking Richard, so she let him be.

When it came to eleven o'clock, Jess was in a quandary; she could not get into her bed, because of Richard, and now Mash was sprawled out asleep on the sofa. Alex's room was of course out of commission, because Mark had not finished decorating the attic; the bed had been dismantled, the mattress upended and put under dust-sheets, and the room was full of paint-pots and step-ladders. There appeared to be nowhere in her own house available for Jess to sleep that night.

This is ridiculous, thought Jess, as she prepared to spend the night in Kate's orthopaedic chair with a quilt around her. But try as she might, she could not get off to sleep, even after such a tiring day. Jess decided she would have to retire to her own bed, if she moved very quietly she would be able to sneak in under the top blanket on the far side of the bed from Richard, who was fortunately still sound asleep. So that is what she did.

Jess and Richard both slept until first light, when Mash awoke downstairs and found that she was cold, so she went in search of warmth, finding it by jumping onto the bed and burrowing her way underneath the blanket.

Richard and Jess woke up. Richard's first thought was "Where am I?" Jess wondered, "Who's this?" and then they both remembered, and laughed.

Also by Jill Robinson:

Berringden Brow – Memoirs of a Single Parent with a Crush

Introducing Jess and her friends, the struggling but still optimistic middle-aged women of a Pennine village, finding themselves having to cope with bizarre job interviews, stroppy teenage kids, ageism, sexism, lookism, sizeism...scanning the personal columns in search of that rare eligible man without hypochondria, a live-in mother, multiple allergies a preference for playing with toy soldiers or a penchant for sex in public places...

But whenever it all gets too much for Jess she can always escape into the library...

"this richly enjoyable, funny and humane read."   Sue Limb

Sons and Lodgers

All Jess wants is a quiet life. All her friends want is somewhere to stay...

Jess feels her serenity slipping as she struggled with teenage tantrums, men's mid-life crises, dope, dogs, refugees, rampant plants, rough sleepers in the shed, bureaucrats on the doorstep- and she is rapidly running out of floor space.

Continuing the everyday story of life in Berringden Brow, not far from Hebden Bridge.

A Place Like This

So many people find their way to the advice centre – asylum seekers, debtors, a trafficked young woman, a heart-broken husband, a man with evil spirits in the house...Jess tries to help everyone, while also contending with the erratic life-style of her son who has embraced freeganism and plastered Hebden Bridge with graffiti. Friends also need her support – but who will help Jess? Meanwhile, why is widowed Norah living in a dog kennel, who has stolen the aspidistra and will Jess's innocent colleague Nick really be sent to prison for conspiring to make a false passport?

The New Forty

Now retired, Jess finds that many people are anxious to call upon her for assistance. Jess wants to help but discovers that her well-intentioned actions are not always appropriate or appreciated.

Meanwhile, a number of interesting opportunities present themselves - stewarding at Glastonbury, volunteering with a children's charity in Romania, appearing on a tea-time TV quiz show and distributing prizes at a writing competition in a haunted barn. Then she finds herself on a storm-tossed cruise ship in the middle of the Baltic with an aging debutante and a young cage-fighter.

On Days Like These

Shouldn't there be more to retirement than making bramble jelly, delivering meals on wheels and contending with the antediluvian attitudes to women of a fellow choir member wonders Jess. Her daughter-in-law suggests various New Age therapies but these are not really what Jess is looking for. Then she is brow-beaten into accepting a free lesson at a celebrity chef's cookery school, before attempting to befriend a trio of rough sleepers camping in the local park in winter. Jess then makes the alarming discovery that her friend Nick may well be the victim of a 'cat-fishing' scheme. Is it really wise for a naive septuagenarian to go chasing off to Colombia to meet the beautiful young Paola, and will she turn out to be who she says she is?

The Rainy Season

1960s small-town Devonshire, where things are far from swinging and Jess must contend with the double standard whereby daughters do housework and their brothers go out to play, and Saturday girls in W H Smith receive threepence per hour less than their male counterparts. A married woman's income is treated as belonging to her husband, and she requires a male guarantor simply to rent a TV set. There is no protection from domestic violence and Jess shares a barricaded bedroom with her depressed mother against the rages of her alcoholic father, who does not believe in education for girls. Jess longs to grow up and escape, but it seems to be taking such an awfully long time...meanwhile the pace of social change is quickening, even in sleepy market towns, and then the Pill becomes available.

Awarded 4 and 5 star reviews on Goodreads and Amazon, this very readable book combines a family story with aspects of the social history of the recent past, still in living memory.

See Facebook Berringden Brow page or email
berringdenbrow@hotmail.co.uk
for further details or to order any of the titles listed.